PRISON SEX

Books by Jacqueline Gay Walley

'Venus As She Ages' Collection of Novels:
Strings Attached (Second Edition, Gay Walley)
To Any Lengths
Prison Sex
The Bed You Lie In
Write, She Said
Magnetism

Books by Gay Walley

Novels:
Strings Attached (First Edition)
The Erotic Fire of the Unattainable
Lost in Montreal
Duet

E-Books on Bookboon:
The Smart Guide to Business Writing
How to Write Your First Novel
Save Your One Person Business From Extinction

Amazon Chap-Books:
How to Be Beautiful
How to Keep Calm and Carry On Without Money

PRISON SEX

A NOVEL

Jacqueline Gay Walley

PUBLICATIONS

Book Three of the VENUS AS SHE AGES *Collection*

I have lived many of the places I write about, many of these characters are based on real people, alive or dead, and I occasionally even use real names, so it is understandable people may think these are real stories. But this book is a work of fiction, because all the events and places got transmuted into a story that the real people would not even recognize. In addition, just as many of the characters are fictitious, the events are fictitious, perhaps even my analyses in the books are fictitious. That said, it bears repeating that nothing in the novel is intended as a recounting of actual events. Apart from the broad parallels, this is not what actually happened to me, nor to the people I write about.

To Peter Miller who has supported me on this journey of knowing that words support the fight for freedom.

LONGING

"What will you do," Mira asks David, as she sits in a black print Spanish dress that swirls round her legs, a tight black sweater buttoned up all the way to her neck, even in this 90 degree heat (you can't show bare arms in prison), "What will you do," Mira repeats to David whose iron-hard thigh she is holding onto, "with your anger when you get out?"

His razor blue eyes look away from her. She takes in his sharp chin, his soft mouth hidden behind his moustache. She is staring at the way he fondles his thoughts, when she hears him say, "I don't know. You'll have to fuck it out of me."

"Sounds bearable," she says, eyes down, looking at her knee. He is too good looking, almost movie star handsome, for her to look at him. It would be too erotic.

Then he gets serious. "I haven't got time to be angry," he says. "I don't believe in that."

"Neither do I," she says, forgetting what it is she does believe in.

She begins to watch another prisoner who has only 12 days left inside. He is in the Gambino family, David tells her. Mira takes in the Gambino man's pristine white t-shirt, his dark close-cropped hair, the hard body, the crisp khaki pants.

She hears David say, "You are looking at a man without any compassion."

She looks back over at the Gambino prisoner about to get out who apparently did some serious things, violent, David tells her, and she watches the Gambino man standing there in the middle of his life, in the middle of this visiting room that looks like a hospital waiting room, waiting for his mother-in-law to come out of the ladies room, while his wife stands anxiously away from him, and Mira in the Spanish dress refuses to believe this man hasn't any compassion.

She raises her delicate face back up to David. "Do you really think we'll get together on the outside?"

He shifts in his chair and nods. "I don't have time to waste when I get out. We're getting together."

Time stops in jail. Even for the visitors.

Mira looks away and can't make sense of this or herself. All she knows is that she is rising, rising with desire everywhere, it's starting to overtake her, her desire for allurement, sexuality, for love, lust, oranges, sand, toes, sandals. It's rising up in her and god knows what will happen if she allows this desire to rise and overtake her, she will start throwing things out of cupboards, she will scream, scream to be loved, she will feel her breasts against her clothes all the time calling to be touched, her sex wet, bedeviling her, time rushing as she stays still.

What she does instead is run her hand primly over the hem of her print dress.

"How did you get this beautiful?" he asks, shifting himself closer to her, rubbing his hand along the back of her perspiring neck, where the sweater does not reach up to.

He rubs her wet neck, and says, "Jesus, it must be 95 degrees in here." He starts kneading her wet neck with intensity.

And her stomach loops in happiness because she knows that if her desire does quiet down on her, goes demure on her, she knows she can always come back to these men jailed and declawed in this barred place of ferociousness. That will wake her up.

Once visiting hours are over, the guards clank the locks shut, and all the colors of the women's pink, white, black, green, yellow dresses, all the strapped, heeled, open toed shoes, all the gold, silver and fake ruby heart necklaces, gold hairclips, white hairbows, pink, red, mauve lipsticks, silver, rope and chain bracelets, all these colors disappear, are left behind in the empty locked-up visiting room. The men refocus their eyes to the monotony of unpainted walls, khaki clothes, the smell of other men, while being strip searched for contraband, one by one before they go back to their cells, insignificantly, because the guards can't confiscate the women's yellow, pink, red and white colors x-rayed into the men's minds before being taken to their cells and locked down, where they will lie on their bunks and some will cry for the disappearance of those free female colors. Some will masturbate to hold on just a little longer to those soft skin tones and curves. Some will simply lie there and go over word for word the conversations with the women. Why didn't they say this or that, why didn't they say what they felt right then, yes they are sorry for fucking up but you liked the money, didn't you? And some will hear the deafening clang of the locks shut all over the prison tonight and, with that sound, they will turn their faces to the wall and tell themselves they don't want it, make her go, make her go away and leave him, shut in. Next time he'll tell her he's busy.

David gets a cigar from the commissary and goes to find his friend Will, who's in for bank fraud, and they go outside and sit on the Bleachers of Truth, and Will and David have a smoke and do a post mortem on their visits.

Will's second wife just left. She's become so thin while he's been down, just had her breasts enlarged so her chest is huge against the smallness of her hips and long legs. Will is thinking about how his wife laughs at everything he says and pats his knee in delight, "Don't think about how it happened, Will. Don't worry about it. Just remember all that we had."

She does not know this is no solace, no solace at all.

David and Will sit on the bleachers and do a little bit of Can We Trust Them Now We Can't See Them? A little bit of reminiscing of trips to the Far East, a little bit of razzing about whose pecs are bigger, who's got less body fat, and as the nights get longer and lonelier, they go onto a little bit of storytelling of women they had and women they didn't.

They can't stop themselves from trying to outdo each other.

Mira is driving home from prison in the rented compact car and plays the radio loud, skips the announcements, so two miles might be classical, then jazz, then soul, then classical. She lights up cigarettes and looks out the window and imagines David sitting next to her, silently taking in the highway lights, Home Depots, refinery and gas stations for the first time in five years. He hasn't heard the sound of an engine rev in almost half a decade. A car horn. He hasn't seen the Statue of Liberty; she's sure, from this angle in New Jersey, never raced past it this way, holding onto it for his very soul.

David throws his cigar down and has Will come with him to Ildefonso's cell because he wants to talk to Ildefonso about cutting his hair. These Spanish guys are good hair cutters. And stand up. They don't lose their women, even in here. They ask

David to help them write their love letters. David always has to say, Cool it man on the sex. Romance them a bit, David says. Don't start talking pussy right after the salutation. David shows them how to compliment the woman on her hair, her last visit, tell her you've been thinking about how wonderful she is.

Ildefonso's got principles, even though he's got that impossible Latin temper which makes him scream anything and then smile and tease the next minute, as if he hadn't just shouted a guy down. And he's pasted a woman's picture up in his cell even though you're not supposed to. David likes that. David likes the rebels. The ones who don't whine and moan about what a rotten deal they have. Those guys are usually rats anyway.

David likes the men who still want to be in the game. Who don't buckle down to authority.

Jesus. You've still gotta live.

David sits outside prison building 5851 in the hot sun. A few lush moments alone. His t-shirt is sweaty but he himself will wash it. He may have to fight someone to keep it this clean, fight not to have the clean t-shirt taken away from him.

David is tired. Earlier he got an air conditioner for a guy so the guy can do a favor for David when he needs one. That's how it is in here. Pay-back. Later he is going to draw a picture of the daughter of a guy in the carpentry shop. He can trade that for wood for his easel.

The women he talks to on the phone tell him to escape in his painting.

And here he is doing representational pictures of the guys' children.

$20 here. $15 there.

He who tried to make all that money outside so he could escape in his painting.

He calls his now ex-wife to hear about what was familiar, to still have a life. She tells him on the phone that she has a headache, she doesn't feel well, here's the kid.

Five years inside and his ex is still angry that he left her to herself.

Mira tells him that what his ex-wife wanted was his passion, but Mira is talking about herself. Mira says love can't grow without passion. The Greek myths point it out all the time, she says. His wife wanted his passion. But most men can't give their wives passion because passion involves waiting, longing, time. You see your wife every day.

That's how wives become prey to other men. They're longing for the imagination of passion.

David remembers when he first met his wife. She was the model at the sculpture studio. She was big breasted and flat stomached and long legged and with her dark eyebrows and long nose, was amazing. Her black hair fell down her back.

They stopped enjoying each other long before he came in. He was too busy. Doing deals. Chasing women who would never know him.

Women are so easy. They want attention. Someone should have told Freud. They simply fall in love with people who love them. It's easy to love a woman, but not your wife. A wife is too angry. Mira says, "Find me a woman who isn't angry and I'll find you a man who isn't a criminal."

"Are you angry?" David asks her.

"Why do you think I'm sitting here with you?" she replies.

David's cellmates tell him to forget his ex. They say, Who wants to go to jail, meaning back to an angry wife. Jail.

David doesn't tell Mira that there are all kinds of passion. Long passion, like he's doing here. Night passion, like he would like to do with Mira. Caring passion, like he has for his wife. All kinds of passion. In fact, every moment is passion.

But he has no passion for the food lines tonight. One hour to get to the food and then they play games with you. Give you one less patty than the other guys because the server is mad about something. It's all so petty and you can't let them get away with it. You can't let them think you're weak. So you say, What the fuck is this man? And so it starts. A lot of screaming. Till you get 4 extra patties. You've gotta hold the line.

When he was out, he would have lost patience with this bullshit. Would have thrown the goddamn food in everyone's face. Here's $100, get me the best table now.

Yeah, the one thing he has learned in here is patience but, god, the food. Bean burritos with beans on the side. He makes lists of menus to amuse himself. The other men are writing about pussy and he's writing about different pastas. Thank God for the Italian guys in here. They find tomatoes, pastas, they cook up a meal. The price you pay is to have to listen to their forced joviality, their camaraderie, their Italian restaurant magnanimity, which he isn't always in the mood for. The fake mafia.

He's saved a tin of tuna. He'll have that. It's in his mattress. That's passion.

He used to call women all the time from phone booths when he was out. When he was on the run. Not on the run from the law but on the run from melancholy, only he didn't know it. He thought he was on the run to freedom. Now he calls Mira twice on Mondays, collect. He knows the hours when there are no lines of men hustling for the phones. Who wants to fight for a goddamn phone?

Mira usually is distracted when he calls. She gets two other calls on call waiting while he's got 10 minutes from the Feds.

Usually he says, "You don't love Big Daddy anymore," because she sounds so busy. She says, "Yes I do" but her voice is unsure.

Today she asked, "When are you getting out of there? I need someone to figure out what's wrong with my Blackberry."

"What's wrong with it?"

"I don't want to talk about it. Just sometimes I need somebody here." Which is unlike her. She is acting out of character. Wants someone to reach her. Hold her. Usually she is as full of bravado as he is. I can take it. I can take anything.

"I'm getting out soon, don't worry," he says. "I spoke to my lawyer. They're changing the marijuana laws. God, these murderers getting out before me. Here I am doing more time than rapists and all I did was give people the munchies. You'll see, the law has got to change. I'll be out in 3 months. Can you handle that?"

She mumbles, "Mm-hmm." She's heard these get-out-quick schemes so much over the last 5 years that she automatically tunes out when he begins to explain a new one. He'll do the time.

She figures he'll do seven or nine. Even though he is more fastidious than a televised lawyer, scouring for every lost clause to prove the judges wrong.

"I need someone to have dinner with. Snails. I feel like snails," she says, nonsensically.

"Well that, baby, you don't have to wait for till I get out."

She smiles. "Okay."

Snails alone, coming up.

He wonders if she likes him crippled like this. Some lovers love like that. She knows where he is at night. When he dreams, she believes it is of her. And if it isn't, she still knows where he is.

He tells her to buy a pink lipstick. The color women wear in porno movies, she notes. He likes the Spanish dresses she wears. Black lace trim round the edges. Black crinoline showing. Spaghetti straps under the sweater.

She's always buying clothes. She likes pretty things. She's a pretty thing herself. However, she frightens him with how much money she can spend. Even when he was earning $54k a week growing marijuana, he was conservative in some areas. He knew where his money went. Only the finest of guns. You can't be a criminal and be frivolous.

"You and violence," she says.

"Look the only violence I want now," he jokes with her, "are blown up photographs of you. So I can paint you."

"I had them taken," she says to him from her desk phone.

"Well I never see them." He is watching a cockroach scurry across the unpainted, unfinished stucco wall next to the phone. He doesn't squash it. Let him go free.

"I don't like the photos. I don't like how I look. Anyway, I sent you one. You know, in black and white."

Yes he knows. He knows it very well. She is staring back at him, her hair lit up in the sunlight, her lips closed, her eyes and mouth slightly smiling. There are lines at the corner of her eyes, her neck has lines, too. She is not young but she is soft, so soft.

He believes that maybe he should be with her when he gets out. She is so soft.

But that's a long shot. Like everything else.

Because she went and did the inconvenient thing, the legal thing if we must be honest, of getting married to someone else when he was on the inside.

"It doesn't matter," she had said, "things will stay the same between us."

"No, they won't," he had answered.

"Yes they will. Look," she said, "I'm in prison too."

Sometimes at night on his cot he goes over the story of her marriage. This is how she tells it. She was living with the man she married before David was sent down. She and this boyfriend had been together for years. Off and on. "At the same time you," she explains to him, "were with your wife and four hundred mistresses."

She keeps on defensively. "I wasn't even close friends with you when you were out." But, as she tells it, she decided to visit David because she knew him in the old days, when they were young, and she lives closer to the prison than his family. His family lives in Massachusetts, she lives in New York, and the Federal Pen is in New Jersey.

She was shocked at the 21 years he got at first. "It was the least I could do for someone I know, visit you," she had said so earnestly.

Florence Nightingale.

So she visited once and, to his surprise, kept coming. He thought the novelty would wear off. All women like the concept of men locked up waiting for them. But he thought that she would tire of the effort, the guards, the indignity. But she did keep coming, once about every three months.

The letters started flying. Collect phone calls became ritual.

Then she told him she was getting married.

"Don't act as if I'm child molesting," she said quickly. "You were married yourself when you were free." Because something changed in here. Five years of letters, phone calls, jokes. Before they knew it they were longing for those letters, phone calls, jokes. They were longing so much, that their lives became entwined.

"Meanwhile, I have to marry him," she had said. "It's the decent thing to do. It's the next step. You're in jail and you won't possibly be there for me when you get out anyway. You're a renowned womanizer. Legendary. There's no woman you've looked at you haven't slept with. You cheated on your wife constantly. People don't change. You think I want to take that on?"

"I'm yours now," he said.

"You're mine because you're locked up."

Meanwhile she's locked herself up with her husband whom David doesn't believe she loves. It is David's and Mira's relationship that is dynamic.

She married her husband out of pity.

Mira asked, "How can you tell the difference?"

Oh god, the things he could teach her. That you can be free in love.

"Free?" she asked. "I wonder how free your wife felt when you were cheating on her."

David hates when Mira dismisses him like this. But who listens to a man doing time? Only the French literary public.

Fuck it, he tells himself, as the sun rises over the top of the electrified fence.

Then there's the woman who visits him whom his ex-wife and Mira don't know about. The guys think Susan is fantastic. Long blonde hair and a straight youthful body. She blooms in the visiting room. If he poured water into her shoes, her petals would stretch out even fuller. Only thing, she talks about astrology and crystals. And she gets angry when the guards take a lot of time strip searching him before he comes out to the visiting room. Susan thinks David is fucking with her, keeping her waiting like that. Like he is master of his time.

Her anger at his being late tells him all she thinks about is herself. It turns him off. He has enough time keeping to do with the guards, not a goddamn blonde woman he's romancing for the hell of it.

That's when he misses Mira, with her dark hair that lights up in the sun and a husband she's saddled herself with.

He tried to tell Mira, "You can't get out. Marriage is quicksand."

"I'll get out."

Mira's like a con, he decides. She thinks she's the only one who will get out. Like all the men here thought they were the only ones who wouldn't get caught. He misses Mira when he's with Susan because Susan's mind is not quicksilver, even though her blonde highlights are.

Susan tells him the minutiae of her life whereas Mira asks him how he feels. Sometimes Mira is silent with him, just holding his hand and that itself is freedom.

At night, when the mail comes, David throws Susan's postcard down on his cot without even reading it. These women think you'll be grateful for anything in here.

The card probably is all about how she picked up the cleaning today and then bought some fresh vegetables. Jesus.

He longs for an intelligent conversation.

He won't get one here. This place is primitive. Men masturbate in front of the TV. They don't care who's there.

Men with some self-respect masturbate in the showers. They say, What happens when a guy gets out of prison and it's raining? Answer: He gets an erection.

Peter, Mira's husband, walks into the apartment. "I'm in my office," she yells from the bathtub.

Peter often wonders why she always takes a bath about the time he comes home. About the time he would want a bath. But Peter kindly says nothing. He knows how much she needs soothing, how much she needs warm water. It's the same with how she sits in the sun continually, skin cancer be damned, "let me be warmed."

Mira, his wife, needs to be touched. Loved. She wasn't loved much as a child, he thinks. Sometimes he feels he can't handle how much she needs. So let her take her baths, sit in the sun, and whatever else she does for warmth. All the phone calls she gets.

Everybody abandoned his little wife, that's what he has to deal with. No mother. A drunk father who dragged her, like a mutt, from bar to bar with him. Propped her up on a dirty bar stool. Then died on her.

Let her take her baths.

She is tainted by desperate memories she rarely talks about. If she does tell him about her childhood, he always feels she is lying. Not telling the real story.

"Scoop!" he yells, for he calls her that because she is like a reporter with the way she takes everything in. She can size up a place in seconds. Just while's he's figuring out which way to hold the menu up, she's figured out the history and future of the place.

She is sweaty from the hot water, and is laying her book down on the wet tiles, as he stands at the bathroom door. Her hair is up but strands fall down wet around her neck. Her breasts are full. She is all woman, he thinks, with the soul of a frightened girl. That's what he sees.

"How was your day at the office?" she asks, joking. He is a carpenter and there is no office. He could not bear an office.

"I made $2000 today."

"Fantastic. That's so much. What happened?"

"Well it's a deposit really on a big job. A staircase."

"Wow. That's marvelous."

"Need any money?" he asks.

"Nope," she says. "You work hard enough."

"When are you going to take something from me?"

"Your youth wasn't enough?"

"Hey," her husband says, "I don't complain."

She laughs. "Give me a bit and I'll get out and you can take a bath."

"Okay."

"Want to see a movie tonight?" she asks. "There's a Russian one that looks interesting."

"We'll see," he said, thinking he would just like to relax a bit before making any decisions.

He goes to the living room to wait for her to come out and lies down a bit.

She's an electric force, he decides. Quick, violent in her passions. She lives on a continual edge of desire. Desire for motion, skirts swirling, for the new. Of course, she wants to go out. Counterphobic to her fear of love. She throws down anything that is repetitive. She is a post-modernist, deciding her values on taste, not reason.

He loves her but, he wonders, can he handle her?

His wife is a self-contained fire and leaves him little to do with himself.

Mira thinks the reason David is doing time is because he killed people in Vietnam and he's paying himself back. She tells herself the reason he allowed himself to do time is that back then he liked the killing. He must be punished.

One of the witnesses at his case testified, "After you kill 80 people in the jungle, you don't really want to come back and drive in the middle of the road."

The judge did not agree. Twenty-one years he gave David. The Rockefeller Drug Laws. Twenty-one years which later was reduced to eleven.

Mira thinks David wanted to get caught.

"What do you think of that idea?" she asks.

David replies, "Could be." He's here, he tells himself, because he couldn't settle down. Some people are meant to burn.

Mira, whom he now considers his mistress although he hasn't been inside her for over twenty years, likes to burn. He can see that. That's why they're meant to be together.

She says she'll be almost 50 when he gets out. "You won't want me."

He says, "Why not? I'll be older, too." She says older men attract young women. "Especially you," she says, "who was, correction who is, so good at attracting women."

"If you want to hide yourself with that excuse, go ahead."

She looks confused.

"Anyway," he continues, "your feet are in concrete."

"What?"

"You're married," he says.

"Oh I'll be out by the time you get out."

She unfocuses her eyes.

Why does he like dark-haired women, he asks himself. Why not Susan who doesn't do the bizarre thing of marrying someone out of kindness, then plans to leave him out of kindness. "He'll want someone normal who can provide more than I can," she explained. What sense is there in that? Why doesn't he like Susan who so easily and eagerly pledges her life to him, rather than Mira who is sometimes harder to get on the phone than the President? She rushes around. Friends, work, theatre, films, music.

David says, "Calm down."

Why not the perfect purity of a blonde? The flawlessness of a blonde? The kind of heartbreaking cut glass beauty of a blonde? Why the tempest of a brunette? You can think a long time in prison.

"What kind of hair does your husband have?" David asks Mira.

"WHAT?"

"What color?"

"Greying dark."

"Ah, an intelligent man."

Mira plays with the button on her sweater, "Not particularly."

He puts his arm around her and says, "And Peter thinks I'm the con?"

Mira tells David that her husband says David should feel guilty.

"Look what David did to his wife and child," Peter points out to Mira.

When she reports this to David, David does get a pang of conscience about his delicate little daughter who jokes with him on the phone. His daughter pretends she's at a fancy hotel and tells him she's the maître d' who's going to find her for him. Oh, here she is.

Hi Dad.

His seven-year-old daughter's face whom he sees round corners for months after a visit. "You shouldn't have grown those plants, Daddy," she says on the phone, meaning the marijuana business that at first got him 21 years. "I'm sending you some money Daddy."

"Oh really, honey, what do you want me to buy myself?"

"Buy yourself?" his daughter says indignantly. "I want you to buy me something."

All you broads are the same, he tells Mira.

Love me.

Mira's husband tells her the prisoner is bad news because he doesn't feel guilty. He's let down the family name. He didn't take care of his wife. Peter says, "Look at the number of guns in his basement. An arsenal."

"I didn't take care of my wife? Jesus when you think of the money I gave her," David responds to her husband's accusations as Mira diligently transports them. Mira is trying to keep her visits a family affair. She is not guilty. "And the government taught me how to use those guns," David went on. "They were licensed."

Mira stares at the wall as if the wall are Peter's accusations.

"I have some guilt," the prisoner croaks up.

"A little?" she asks.

"A lot," he says. Although he is not sure for what. He just shouldn't be here.

He looks over at his buddy Will who has someone's wife whom he didn't know on the outside visiting him. Someone's wife who thinks she's doing a good deed. Aren't women out there getting enough attention?

———————————————————————

Her husband calls her from his other house, the one in the country. She doesn't go there much with him, except when it is summer and she wants to be outside. The house doesn't have a garden and that is something she can't keep from noticing.

Mira has never liked the house he was building when she met him, the house Peter claims he built for her but he hadn't known her when he started it.

It is true that part of her husband's attractiveness had been that he owned a house. He was tangible. He would outlast time. She would have a home with him. A home to come home to. Mira's mother took off when she was a baby and her father and she roamed from bar to bar, motel room to motel room.

She watches him sanding a floor and feels love for him. His artistic long slender body. His warmth. He can be stubborn and contrary at times, but who isn't? She loves his humor and how he is always kind to people. She loves that he likes to be busy. She loves how he has a quality of true north. He would never lie or cheat. He is too honest.

He is beautiful. He is good. And maybe he is just too good for her.

"Will's not worthy of that woman who visits him," Mira tells David as she watches Will and the clean-cut married woman who is sporting a huge diamond on her wedding finger. Mira studies them sitting over there at the next row of chairs. "Will's in here for partying hard and then believing he was invincible signing his life away to some real cons that let him take the fall."

David nods.

But what he's thinking is that Mira is wrong. You don't make the kind of money Will made without knowing you were doing some kind of crime. But he likes Will. Will is the only one in here who has at least put some missions together and seen something of the world. Most people are petty criminals. David likes the people with long time. They could take it out there and they can take it in here. Not these babies looking for a place to stay for a year.

"Why don't you go down to the infirmary?" Will says later that night to David who has a bad cold.

"And wait 6 hours for them to give me an aspirin? Forget it. I don't believe in that shit."

"You look awful."

"Will, my man," David says, "your trouble is you've been pampered."

"Hell, Daaave, I'm all for pampering."

"I am too. But a prison doctor is not my idea of pampering. I can come up with some better ideas." David coughs. "Jesus I can't even have a cigar."

"Any news from Mira?"

"She says she's sick of men. I guess guys bother her at the gym or call her up for stuff. Who knows?"

"What did you say?" Will asks in his Kansas twang.

"I told her I was sick of men too."

On their next visit, David tells Mira he would like her to sit on him. She says she would like it too although she doesn't tell David she is bored with her husband in that way. She looks away and wishes she had a cigarette so she could push away the thought that she might even be bored with David that way.

But right now it's not an issue.

David tells her how he's always thinking about when she will pick him up when he leaves here. How they'll call him in to the warden's and say, You're free. And then he'll call her up on the phone to come get him. And then he'll just sit outside on that green, soft grass, and wait, deliciously, smelling the breezes, with no one looking over him, for her to come from New York.

He thinks about how she will sit on him in the car.

She, in her turn, amuses herself by planning what she will wear when she picks him up (a black velvet evening dress, strapless, with a slit. She doesn't bother to wonder if she still fits into it.) She wonders which restaurant she will take David to for his first gourmet meal in 8 years, what a soft bed with fresh sheets will feel like to him. The rose that comes in with the breakfast tray, will he take a second and lose himself in it?

She imagines the aesthetics she will shower David in, a perfect fresco she creates, but behind that fresco, she nervously feels the memory of her husband, Peter, picking her up from the airport ten years ago and how they drove into the mountains of New Hampshire, she can't remember why now, but the thought that he might have desired another woman while she was away, was so erotic and painful to her, that she had to cross over the stick shift and got on him hungrily and wildly. She had to do that. Peter was a little confused, why didn't she want to wait till they were in the motel room? But the pain of his being gone and the possibility of his even thinking of another woman drove her mad so she had to now claim him, he is hers, in the car in the motel parking lot.

That was then.

She shudders. Will that happen when she picks this one up? Will she be driven by the same furious, frightened desire? Fueled by the same pain of having been possibly abandoned?

She looks around the prison visiting room. Maybe the bars on those tiny box-like prison windows are staving off her fury. She looks blindly outside and continues thinking about the red roses that the room service man will bring with their breakfast tray in to their first hotel room, the exact timing of the bloom.

How David will linger on it.

She will be divorced by then because her husband will know that she is worthless. He will want a decent woman by then. Someone who knows how to love.

She will be free for a criminal.

She looks over at David's large hard body. His exquisite blue eyes. Blue eyes. Her father told her never to trust a man with blue eyes. Her father had hazel eyes and he couldn't be trusted so all eyes are the same.

What she loves about David is that this time she'll have someone to contend with.

Truth is, she frightens Peter with that ugly fury of hers.

She grips David's knee tight. She wants to believe she can't frighten this man.

It's such a burden when a woman frightens a man.

"I want my mommy," a lot of the guys start saying in here. They say it joking of course.

And then dial their wives.

Some of the wives refuse the collect call.

But the real mommies always take the calls and always visit. David's can't, his mommy is dead. But these mommies visit and sometimes one of them stops Mira in the waiting area and tells Mira her son was set up. Her son is innocent. He was framed. He was loaning out his garage.

Mira always remarks to David how fresh faced the men look. How youthful. She believes it is the mommies who keep these men young. You have no responsibility, honey. Just love me.

Yes there's all that crime talk about dysfunctional homes. These boys didn't get enough love. But some of these boys got too much love in Mira's opinion. Blind love. You can do anything-you-want love as long as you stay-by-me love. That's negligence too.

David is watching Mira look around the room and sees her not trusting the mothers even. Jesus, this woman trusts no one, he tells himself, It's her defense and David gets tired of it, always telling him he's a womanizer, he won't want her, cross examining him the way she does about his ex-wife. He gets tired of it, but she's right, he is a womanizer.

Mira doesn't want to be conned. All he can think is that someone must have done a good job at one time on her. She's a walking electronic eye. But he's always liked a challenge. Easy women are boring.

Mira makes it seem she's worth the effort. At least he believes so now.

What David tells her is that their conversations after five years inside are stagnating. They don't do anything together and he doesn't do much anyway so where can their conversations go.

They're running out of things to talk about.

Like a woman, she thinks that's literally impossible. What she says is, "Don't worry about it. I know we don't do anything together."

She dismisses him because how can anyone run out of things to talk about if they're seducing each other?

So what he does is ask her to dress sexy during the visits. She resents that, she's middle aged for one thing. She resents his wanting her to dress sexy because she finds it hard under the constraints. Do you tell someone in the mid-east to dress sexy? She has to wear a bra in here and no arms can show anyway and she doesn't have great legs, she says. They seem fine to him especially with what he's had to look at for five years.

You can't bring lipstick in and she doesn't like to kiss him on the first half of the visit because her lipstick will be gone and then that's that. He knows that's why she turns her head the first half of the visit and it makes her nervous that he can see into a woman like that. It makes her nervous that he's capable of putting himself into another's shoes. A woman's particularly. He likes high-heeled shoes. So does she.

It makes her nervous because most men can't put themselves into a woman's shoes, or won't, and this makes him far more dangerous than any goddamn arsenal found in his basement.

Somebody should get a little insight about the danger in that.

MASTURBATION

Masturbation, in this situation, is all. Her husband, she tells the prisoner, goes traveling and comes back with Playboys in his suitcase. "Don't get upset," her husband says, "I've been using them for years."

The guys inside, of course, use pictures, too. Or they sit in front of the TV. Anything, the evening news, works. The movies the guards show the prison population are violent, shoot 'em ups, thieveries. Not pornographic.

"That's crazy," she says. "Why would they be that stupid?"

He tells her the guards want the inmates to get excited. A riot provides $40/hour overtime for them.

Her face scrunches up at that.

He goes into the showers. Not exactly with her. It's amazing what stuff you get into when you're masturbating. It does become almost any woman, faceless, sitting on you on the stairs, her back to you. Control. Look you don't exactly walk into this stall in a perfumed fantasy. The place stinks, there are guys waiting for the stall, guys who drive you fucking crazy. Sure you can start out all romantic in a way in your fantasies but when things get going, all that ends and it's just rough fucking and release. Images of blowjobs, long blonde hair streaming around the nameless head up and down. Pushing her. Pulling her. Up and down. Hurting her.

Probably she's got full breasts but they're hidden because her face is covered, like a criminal's. She's just another person who's fucking you and whom you're fucking. She's got a full ass if he must picture it. Why women all want to be so skinny no one does it in their head with a woman who looks like a boy but when it comes down to it you're not looking at them anyway.

He asked Mira to rent a movie with Nikki Dial who has enthusiasm for blowjobs so she'll see what he likes but she says she's embarrassed asking since she knows the video guys.

"They'll respect you," he tells her. "They'll think you have good taste."

She doesn't tell him the video guys are gay and into crystals and herbology, members of a witch sect.

She doesn't tell him he has a fantasy of what it's like out here.

Her sexual fantasies are mostly watching her husband or some man with a 10-inch cock and another woman have a great time. She watches and mutely, off camera, participates in their giving over. She is never, ever made love to in her erotic fantasies and David's sure she's never told her husband that.

She sends him erotic stories she's written but it's she, not the stories, he finds erotic. He finds the way she moves quickly, neatly, totally feminine, her large lips erotic. Her voice and the way it hums at the end of a sentence, especially when she's nervous.

He finds her shyness erotic, as if she is there for him to spoil.

She says she has to masturbate almost every night to go to sleep. Sometimes in the afternoon if she's tired or anxiously waiting for anything to happen. Her fantasies are never violent; in fact they sound fairly clean and proper. The woman isn't exactly vanquished, the woman isn't raped, no she is just amazed, it seems to him, at the manliness of the man.

Now that he's asked her to notice her sexual fantasies, she can't fantasize as well, she says.

She needs secrecy. She told him that some psychologist wrote that intellectual, sexually inhibited women fall for men in prison.

He dismissed it. Irrelevant, your honor. The woman he's fantasizing about couldn't possibly be sexually inhibited. He isn't doing time for that. She's pretending she's repressed is what it is. It's her cover. They both know that sooner or later someone's going to open the fucking door.

He only hopes it's him.

It's getting harder when she visits. She came in a tight red sweater, with an open v-neck, god knows how she wore that in, but he was able to run his hands up and down the beginning rise of her breasts. Eyes in back of his head for the guards.

He pulled her leg up over his knee to see the shape of it. He is tired of this place. He wants release and right now that means he wants her.

Mira has noticed a change in herself. Lately she stays longer with herself, in her fantasies. Longer with herself as the recipient of the erotic pleasure. She doesn't switch to the other woman so fast. Lately she has been walking and feeling inexplicably happy. She needs no one. The entire play is within her. Lately she is friendly to anyone who calls or runs into her. She is at her own festival. She is happy, free.

She tells David this and it makes him nervous for does this not mean she won't want a locked up man for much longer?

"Be careful how you use your time," he tells her.

"What do you mean?"

"Don't fritter it on thousands of things."

Mira knows he means, don't get distracted by some other man, but she asks, "What do you mean?"

"Focus on your work," he says.

Meaning him? she wonders.

David does not find sex a soporific, what with it having to take place in the shower here, the only place you can somewhat be alone. They wake you at 5 am and march you down for a urine test for drugs, and they stand there and watch you pull your dick out. That's intimacy now.

"Why don't you do it in your bed?" she asks when he complains about the dirt in the showers.

Like girls do.

"I'm not alone in my bed. There are 10 other guys in the room."

"Be quiet," she says, like girls do in boarding schools.

"It's messy, honey. It's a different thing."

He laughs.

She says confidence and creativity are drained out of her.

She's not good at juggling men. Christ, he can't imagine that. He had three changes of clothes in his car in case he had an unexpected sleep over. And he always had unexpected sleepovers.

"Didn't you feel guilty?" she asks.

She has seen him when she does it with herself, seen him with some beautiful blonde bank teller who watches him put his $54,000 in a safety deposit box weekly and soon the blonde is bent over the desk and he's fucking her, partially to once again fuck the law but also the blonde.

Mira gets confused. Undoubtedly she is an outlaw too, to get mixed up with him but she doesn't have the fun that real outlaws have. It wouldn't be fun for her to fuck some bank teller. Whom would it be fun to fuck? She has no idea.

She wishes it was her husband she could open up with and sometimes she gets into bed hoping she'll be free, and there have been times she's been free, but that's when she's been thinking of the guy in jail who makes her feel free. That's because he gives her freedom. Her husband doesn't like her feeling free. He yells at her to feel free.

Jesus what a mess. A mess is never really erotic.

What is erotic? Danger for some reason. Is that because women feel the pulse of their fathers' danger and men feel the rush of their mothers' blonde perfection?

Only a partner like that now.

The unavailable partner that our hearts crack a little open for. Shut tight for your husband.

"If your heart is broken," she tells David, "you can't do anything." Her heart is broken.

"Why baby?"

"I don't know."

Meaning she doesn't have the volumes to tell him.

And that is her mistake. If she told him the volumes, her heart would open. Her very own heart.

She is the one masturbating with her heart. In silence.

Mira works alone. She writes articles making companies look good. Sometimes she goes for days without seeing anyone except her husband. All her assignments and interviews are over the phone. She is disciplined, focused, turns her work in on time.

A big event for her is getting lunch to go from the health food place. People try to pick each other up there but they never try to pick her up. She is too wild looking, unhealthy with her red lipstick and high heels, amid all this granola. Being way past forty, she is too old.

She comes back upstairs to work. Plays a Te Deum and waits for something to happen.

This is her passion.

David says his dreams are erotic but Mira's dreams lately are of being a nun. Longing and masturbating.

Last night in the cab she longed for her father. But when she thought about it, she knew it was not really her father. She was just longing to love as passionately as the little girl does for her father. With such trust and fervor. Oh she wants that ecstasy, that transcendence. Of course she dreams of being a nun, everybody, including herself, is busy betraying themselves.

David tells her his sexual fantasy is her sitting on his lap, and then she gets up to dress and he undresses her, and then she is sitting on his lap again.

What does that tell, she wonders. It's not particularly erotic to her; it's more about his getting her to do what he wants. "What does it mean?" she asks.

"You desire me is what it is," he explains impatiently.

Will she accept nothing on faith?

"You choose to be with me."

"That's erotic?" she asks.

"Yes."

Yes, she thinks, for a powerless man.

"Your sexual fantasy?" he asks.

She forgets. "Life is too complicated by sadness," she says.

Neither of them search out porno books or magazines anymore. Only her husband does.

It's her husband who wants the perfect simplicity and silence of a freshly printed picture.

Mira and David have telephones, electric and barbed wires to skew them.

"Would you prefer a sensual lover, an aggressive loud lover, or a dominatrix?" she asks.

"Sensual," he says, knowing that's how she sees herself. "I like a woman," he says, "who sometimes likes to take control."

"You like oral sex don't you?" she asks.

"I prefer to give it. Most women don't do it very well anyway."

She listens.

"It's too much work for me," she says.

"Well I like to give it. I'm incredibly oral," he replies.

She knows she is supposed to be turned on by that thought but she isn't. Even receiving it seems like too much work. She would have to be present to him. To herself. It frightens her.

She had thought while she was driving here that being in love, letting go, is the main event of life. You do your work, and it's better if it's a passion, it should be, but loving someone is the joy, the whipped cream and the depths of the sea, yet here she is holding herself back from everyone.

And here he is being held back. Somehow there is more dignity in that, she tells herself. He has no choice. But she does.

He even had the courage to love her while doing time. Given her enough love to rope her into these visits. But she? Whom does she give herself to?

"I'm going to need some help falling in love," she says.

"It just happens, like it did with me for you."

She looks at him and doesn't believe him. Isn't love earned? Yet he believes it just happens. He's looking for it, wants in.

She smiles at him fondly. Smiling at him fondly is the best she can do.

"I love even the thought of you," he says. "It's what gets me through."

David of course has no sensuality anywhere around here.

He could bring in beautiful women to impress people and himself but what's the point. Everyone bores him except Mira. He'd rather be with a woman who smiles full lipped and generously when he comes out of the locked in waiting area than someone with a perfect hourglass figure. Of course, both would be good but actually he would take a woman happy to see him, and Mira is happy to see him no matter what she says. He'd rather have that than some model who is angry that he's not looking at her enough.

He's lost the hang of desiring a roster of beautiful bodies anyway. He never sees beautiful bodies now except for men's. And they don't interest him. Some of the guys here, especially those with long time, and not usually the white guys, they take a lover among the inmates. That leads to fights. They might kill their lover just for witnessing their sexual indignity. Some of the female guards aren't bad to look at but jesus, all the paraphernalia they wear. The pants and the handcuffs and the sticks. The bus driver shirt tucked in over fat waists.

They make a point of hiring ugly women in prisons. And if they're pretty, the women put on a lot of weight.

Talk about killing desire.

Everyone who visits him, even the minister from his hometown, asks him if he misses sex in prison. Could anyone even imagine a more stupid question?

But David always answers patiently. If it gives these visitors a thrill to talk about his confinement, let 'em have it. Gives these visitors a thrill that finally, finally they are sitting with someone who is more confined than they are.

So David says, "It's the tenderness you miss."

"God," Mira says, "how we scurry about for tenderness. I can't figure out what to masturbate to anymore."

"That's because you don't want to be the voyeur and you don't want to participate."

"Now what happens?"

"You act. You jump in. But wait for me."

Could she masturbate to herself being made love to?

He looks askance at her. And this is the woman who is feeding me in here?

The next morning she puts on makeup she bought the night before very carefully. She brings her deep-set eyes forward. Smooths out her skin. She combs her hair out softly. She is not sure for what. For something unexpected. She hopes. For herself as woman.

He does another day of difficulty and dryness in jail.

Putting on makeup for nothing but hoping it's something is masturbation too.

Her husband takes on construction jobs out of town. And buys Playboy.

Her husband occasionally tells her that she has let him down. She rarely cooks a meal, she somehow believes it's cheaper to eat out in New York when you count the time you spend cooking.

She won't blend their finances. She is generous but insists on her own account. He tells her he's furious she won't have a child. He may leave her unless she has one.

However, he calls her every night.

He does not let her down.

David sends her a page torn out of a magazine with a pair of Ferragamo sandals on it. High heels, ankle straps. "Do you like these?" he writes.

She feels inexplicably lonely. She is relating only to surface. To buy the shoes would be messy. It would make her longing vibrant. The heels would click along the street, for no one whom she could touch.

David calls his ex-wife. A woman he slept with for fifteen years. A woman who bore his child. David feels Mira is wrong not to have a child, but she didn't have enough love to have a child. Her husband is as wounded as she is.

Her husband wants her to be his mommy and you can't have a baby with your baby.

David doesn't want a mommy. David's ex-wife is strong, aggressive, like him. It makes them competitive with each other and angry but his ex is someone to be dealt with, not protected. While Mira lives an emotional subterranean life, his wife bellows out the moment. He has no idea whom he is more compatible with and it doesn't matter. All he has now is masturbation and frankly it's with neither of them that he comes. It's just the faceless, nameless fuck.

"Tell me any sexual fantasy," Mira asks him over the phone. "Not one about me. Any, any . . . ," she says driven almost to madness. This is a woman who cannot be touched except by her own madness.

"Is there a shadow coming over Manhattan?" he asks her on the phone.

"You mean because you have an erection . . .?"

"It's your voice," he says, "your voice that excites me."

David sneaks out a roll of film to Mira. She has them developed and they are pictures of himself. On the laundry machines.

At the staircase. In his cell. Smoking cigars. On the phone. Mugging with two of the other guys. Strip-teasing. One of him nude going into the shower. One of him sitting in the shower holding Mira's picture. A joke between them.

It makes her uncomfortable.

Twenty shots of him that she flips through as she walks from the photo-processing place. She smiles at the photos, his physical attractiveness. He is alive in her hands.

He knows he is physically attractive. She would never feel that comfortable about herself to send an undeveloped roll of film of herself to anyone.

Her friends say, "What are you Doing with a Guy in Jail?" till she shows them his picture and then they say, "Oh yeah I get it."

"He'll break my heart," Mira says.

"Yeah, honey, but look at it this way. You get him on the first night he's out of jail."

Mira laughs.

She is amazed at the generosity, the realness of these pictures. Twenty shots of David.

He is open.

The cleaning man who comes to Mira's house wears a beige cardigan and looks like a Professor. David's tall good looks and ocean eyes make him appear a movie star yet he is in jail. Her husband's tall slender darkness is that of a poet and he is busy telling everybody to make money.

Mira goes round the apartment staring at photos of her husband. In the ones he is alone in, he glares at the camera. Which means he is glaring at her because she took the photo. In the ones of them together, he grabs her, his arm reigning her in tight. She seems always to be running away.

Her husband, the poor guy, might have been masturbating with her all these years.

My heart is breaking, Mira says to no one, no one at all, my heart is breaking for my husband.

Who would want a criminal like me?

"Can you handle me baby?" David asks Mira. "I'm going to be crazy when I get out of here."

Oh God, she thinks, have you got it wrong who's crazy here.

What is it that stops us all from making love with each other? she wonders.

The Freudian shrink tells her that it's not expressing enough anger.

The Jungian says it's not being in your authentic journey. Being isolated from yourself. How can you make love to another if you're not making love to yourself?

David says it is entrapment that stops everything.

His ex-wife doesn't see what the problem is. Just make love. Goddammit.

Mira's husband thinks it's not enough submissiveness. It's women's eternal rebelliousness. If they would just get strong enough to say Yes.

Mira thinks it's fear of engulfment. If you give yourself to someone who loves you, they will smother you. Kill you. Or worse, let you down.

David listens to this.

Then she said, "I was with a client. And I read a note I wrote to him. The note said, "I will bill you at the end of the month." But when I reread the note, I thought I had written, "I will kill you at the end of the month."

"Did you tell him?"

"No. Why let him know what's really on my mind?"

"I used to use the sun," she said, "to help my fantasies. Most of my sexual fantasies take place on the beach. It's been so long since my husband and I made love on the beach."

"How long?"

"Years. The thing is you stop trying with your husband. Oh I'm committing such a crime. Not trying with him better."

"You shouldn't have married him."

She doesn't say, I would commit the same crime with you. And right there, because she keeps silent, she commits the same crime.

Aloneness.

Even though she loves David, she misses the sight of her husband. David is not familiar to her. When she sees a man in a woolen winter cap like the one her husband wears, she misses her husband. When a man in a duck jacket the same shape and make as her husband's come out of a store, she misses her husband. She knows all of her husband's clothes. She is intimate with his movements, his walk, his smile, or lack of one, the foods he chooses, his shoes, his fire. It will be the beginning of the end when she no longer knows what shoes he wears. She is not intimate with her husband as she should be but she is intimate with everything about and around him.

She knows nothing of David's shoes or jackets. Once she snuck him in a grey sweatshirt. She sees in the photographs that one of the other inmates is wearing the sweatshirt. Maybe it was the wrong size for David. Maybe David all along had planned to give it the other inmate.

David frequently calls her and asks her to send $10 to another inmate, a man who has no one sending him in anything. He asks her to send fudge to the girlfriend of yet another inmate.

David wants everybody to be happy. Except those whom he was intimate with.

No, writing is not masturbation, Mira explains to David. Even though everyone seems to be writing as much and easily as masturbation. Everyone's got their hands on a pen.

But writing is supposed to be talking to someone. Yes, they may not hear.

But it's supposed to be two-way.

What is this? A world of autoeroticism, like children. Don't you see, David? You put yourself there so you would not have to bear the responsibility of loving. So you can masturbate there, not bear the responsibility of mature loving.

David gets a frightened look on his face like Mira is turning into a wife.

Aha, she thinks, he is not really up for me.

THE VISITS

First you fill out a form saying you're not bringing in fire-arms and drugs. Now who, Mira wonders, would check Yes, May I take these explosives through?

Then you lock your handbag in one of the gym lockers, put the last touches of makeup on before you do that. You keep putting make up on as you wait to be processed, to quell the anticipation so that you end up walking into the visiting room looking a little like Gloria Swanson on a bad day. You put the $1 and $5 bills they let you bring inside in your coat pocket. You take anything else you had in your coat pocket out. You check that your bra straps won't show when you take your coat off inside. That no cleavage shows. You loosen your slacks so the guards don't think they're too clingy.

Then they look at your driver's license, look up in their files to see if you've been approved by the Feds, meaning you're not an ex-felon yourself. You lean over the counter to see what other women are visiting David, but the guard keeps a close hand over David's file, so you don't see anything. Then the guard asks you to walk through the metal detectors that pick up static even in your shoes. Everything makes that detector ring. You take your jewelry off. You take your shoes off. Little kids, in high prank form at the imminent joy of seeing their fathers, cheer for everyone when the metal detector finally shuts up.

The guards go through your pockets. Then you put your jewelry and shoes back on and they stamp something that doesn't show in normal light but vibrates under another metal detector.

"Why?" she asks the guard.

"Only people who have the stamp come out."

As if anyone could fit into this blouse.

Finally you've put all your paraphernalia back on, it's been checked, and then you wait in a locked hallway while they take a long time to process the other mothers, lovers, wives, brothers and stool pigeons waiting to come inside. Then another guard comes in holding paperwork and you and the guard stand there officiously waiting for a person behind locked windows to electronically unlock the door to take you and the guard through to another locked door where you wait for it to be unlocked electronically, then another, again, another, again.

Then the guard holds the door and you're in the visiting room. Guards are sitting at TV monitors and marking on a sheet of paper which inmate came in, which inmate went back. They write in slow motion, like they are children rounding out big C's in handwriting class. Mira wonders if David is right that the guards are as mentally impaired as he says.

Mira sits down with the other people just let in and waits for her prisoner. Must be like asking for someone at a peep show. "And now after screwing 1000 women and never getting tired just back from a long hiatus where he was saving up on testosterone…"

While she waits, she looks at the people. Mostly women come.

Some men have very pretty women with soft hair done up with combs, women with slight figures in tight skirts, women with clear skin that shows no pain. They have them visit. Just to show them off.

Others don't care about showing anybody off. They'll have any woman who's been approved by the FBI and is willing to, visit. They're just glad to see someone of the female sex, even their mothers will do.

The women who aren't lookers sequester themselves down deep in chairs and wait. An hour from now, Mira will see them sitting in the same position, in silence, next to their inmate. A hand draped over their man. The man will keep looking nervously away.

Each prisoner is allowed only a certain amount of visits. The women on welfare come visit as often as the prisoner point system allows. It's what they do. They get up and go to prison. They sit there in their baggy shirts and skirts, legs bare and in flat sandals, and kill time. They watch the kid. The inmate says hi to other inmates.

Pretty women tend to strut. Are more ready to smile one woman to the other. This is a lark, baby. Don't forget it. I got plenty of men on the outside. But everybody loves a bad boy, don't we.

A disturbing amount of the women are pregnant.

Mira breaks her reverie to see David make his manic entry from the prisoners' locked door into the visiting room. It's like making an entrance on a stage; there is that much solitary space between the locked door and where he has to give his visitor's pass to the guard.

David quickly looks Mira over.

In a second, he annotates what he and the other guys must be taking in: she's between a looker and ordinary. She once was a looker so she carries some of that strut. But her face is tired now. Some of the inmates catch the strut.

Mira and David never talk right away. He is taking her in, he says. His eyes have to adjust to her neck, her eyes, her mouth, her legs, her feet, all of her. Always a new visual. He has to feel it, take it in.

Finally, he opens with the lines. The same lines he has used on women for years.

"How did you get this beautiful?"

Mira is bored with those lines now.

"Don't start with that."

"Baby, how are you doing?" he says laughing.

She touches his hair. She always notices his haircut. She thinks this latest barber is fantastic. A great cut. How can she get an appointment?

"What do you like about it?" David asks.

"It shows off your face. It's shorter. More of a man's cut. Not a man trying to be a boy."

"Did they give you a hard time?" he asks her. Meaning the guards.

"They always, always make us wait."

"Man, that's what it's all about," he says. "That's part of the punishment."

The visiting room is sexy, let's face it. Bulls let out into the pit. The cows waiting. Okay, you can't do anything but just the primitive, paleontological connection of the survival of the fittest, the bad bulls let into the pen. These men buck authority, the women right there with them.

These aren't the really, really bad bulls. The really really bad bulls die, hang themselves up, hang themselves.

It's sexy in here because sex is repressed. Everyone is penned.

Maybe it's the woman's inverted power, she gets to buy him food in the vending machines, she holds the money, she is on top, maybe in a way it's that she can't bring makeup in and what that means is that eventually she's going to look like she would in bed anyway, maybe it's just all the pent up desire that fills up the room and everyone shares it, even the guards.

The food is awful. Cellophaned sandwiches. Mira won't even have one. She always has popcorn, like she is at the movies. Maybe it is a movie for her.

He has a steak sub, plastic food but it's a celebration. At least there isn't a line for it, at least it doesn't come with rice and beans, which they serve on the inside for every meal, even breakfast. There are ice creams here, cheesecake in wrappers. Even a cappuccino machine that is usually broken. She has that, but of course she's worried about her lipstick coming off.

It's awkward. If his hand is going too eagerly, too emphatically round the bareness at her back, the guards motion him over to them. He knows this could mean a mark in his file. It could prolong his time. If he kisses her, same thing. He's more careful now than he used to be.

There have been times he's unhooked her bra and felt her breasts but it all depends on the administration and right now the guards are tough. She can't even drape a leg over him. She can't stand with her back to him at the vending machines. It's too much like the position in bed. He can't put his arms round her.

They hold hands sometimes. They take furtive serious looks at each other. But actually they're two people who like to talk and tease and perhaps, she wonders, they are not that sexual anyway. Because they can talk and he paints, they have release. They have other vehicles than sex so it's not important to become figure eight bodies in the visiting room. It's just the tenor of voice differences and her smallness against his shoulder and the little jokes.

This visit lasts 6 hours. For some reason, he tells her the truth about his life. I mean how many lies can you tell in that long a stretch. You have to be able to get away to tell lies well. He tells her that his wife used to get angry when he used her comb or he touched one of her books. He tells her that going for a walk with his wife was like bringing a trailer with you; she had that much baggage in her mind before she'd hit the road. He tells her his wife didn't know he was sleeping with all her friends.

Mira listens quietly.

He admits to the lines he gives women about how incredible looking they are. Mira knows how easily they work, how easily they worked on her.

He tells her he's going to be monogamous with her. They both find that an overwhelming thought and as he tries to believe his promise as he is saying it, he feels he is going to pass out. Has he ever talked this long to a woman without any props? No sexual contact, no pretty clothes, no liquor, no beaches, no movement? Just harsh lighting and terrible food and guards watching them and them talking, talking.

"We're covering a lot of ground here," he says.

She is dizzy too but some of it is knowing they can't walk out the door together. It's only in her dreams that they do normal things like go to a café, walk through Central Park, decide to go to a movie on a whim. Her eyes keep running to the tiny barred up window and the Canadian geese flying over as David talks.

David watches her face. He knows what's going on there. She's telling herself he's bad for her, she will be his wreckage. Yet like all women, she wants to pass him the matches.

David watches her looking out the window.

"You're the one who wants to stay in prison," he says, to start a healthy fight. "You don't want to believe I can make you happy."

How could he? she asks herself. It takes a selfish man to go to prison.

"I don't even know you," she says. "You're going to be completely different when you get out."

"You know what?" he says, "what you see here. That's who I am. There'll just be more of me."

Is that what she wants? More of him? She shifts on the chair.

"I feel a little faint," he says. "Too much truth."

"You can lie a lot when you get back to your cell. Balance your blood sugar out."

He laughs. "Yeah. I'll tell them right away you're my sister and I'm fucking you."

"Good," she says, "just keep lying. You'll feel like your old self in minutes."

Mira is at home now at her desk. Her husband is out of town, building. She buys 2 tickets to a concert, not knowing whom to invite. Benny Carter, old swing music. Happy music. After she gives her credit card number to the telecharge, she is not sure why she did this. Already she misses sad music.

She also doesn't like the open feeling of not knowing whom she will ask to go with her. That makes her uncomfortable. Maybe it's a sign she wants to fall in love. Some man will run into her on the street. She can't think of any woman to invite. She doesn't want the swing music interrupted with anti-ex-husband soliloquys. So she calls a man she knows, a man who bores her, in truth, he always states the predictable. But it's better for her to go out with men that she cannot love. That way she is free for her husband. Or David.

Or something unknown.

The boring friend accepts her invitation too willingly, like he is a dog who is supposed to be fed. I'll take it. She feels rage once he accepts. He has never taken her anywhere. Wouldn't think to ask her to something, make her happy. Another locked up man, one who has locked up his originality, who has nothing to offer.

She doesn't even know anyone else whom she could have asked to the music. Whose own life is light. Is anyone's? The lighter, healthier men are married. The lone dogs are dark, uncompromising. Depressing, if truth be told.

She is angry that here she is, with another man whom she is transporting music to, to save them. Save both her and the man.

He doesn't deserve her. None of these men do. She brings them music and they bring her their chains. Clank clank clank. Beat beat beat.

David isn't calling lately. Sometimes he just doesn't want to talk to anybody out there. Nobody understands what he's dealing with in here anyway. The easiest way to do the time is not to be in contact with the outside world. This always works for a while and then you get a fucking spring day. A day that's a little warmer. And then it starts. You can feel in your veins what it's like to fire up your truck. You remember coming over a hill with a grey somber sky that as you drove began to open up blue on you. Your heart wants to start breathing large, not like a shut up dog. You remember what it's like to put your hands round a woman's waist and over her breasts under her blouse. Your hands over the warmth up her skirt. Your desire starts rustling. It's warm out and the earth smells and you start remembering what it was like to stand up against the chrome of your truck and have the whole day to feel in love or look for stained glass windows or have your toddler daughter repeat everything you say. The air is warmer and everything stirs up.

That, that, takes you to the phone. He calls Mira collect. She's not there. He calls Susan. She's not there. It's warm. They're all out. He calls his ex-wife, his daughter. They're not there. He calls his brother. No one home. He calls Mira again. She's home.

"What's the matter?" he asks.

"I bought tickets to a concert and I asked this idiot to go with me. And I just figured out why."

"Why?"

"Because when I go alone, when I'm alone," and here she hesitates, "when I drive home in the cab alone, I start to miss my father. I start begging him to return to me. I start longing for that passion, that ecstasy I felt for him. You know, when I was around

3 or so. And then I get all emotional and then I realize it's not my father I'm missing at all. I wasn't THAT close to my father after I was little. What I'm missing, are you ready for this . . ."

"Okay . . ."

"I begin to realize I'm missing God. Get it? So I buy two tickets to a concert with no one to go with because I don't want to be alone. I don't want to start missing God."

He hesitates. He waits a second. He can see the sun out of the window by the phones, lighting up the prison yard. It almost looks pretty.

"What am I talking about?" she asks.

"What are you talking about?" he repeats, "I don't know."

She sounds so sad. Why is she so sad when she's out there, free? She thinks he knows what she's talking about. She thinks he knows about God because of all the people he killed in Vietnam and he watched be killed. 29 deaths counted. Probably more like 150, he always says jokingly. Doesn't bother me at all, he laughs it off. No, doesn't bother me at all, I just let myself go to prison. She thinks he knows about God.

Why is she going to music with an idiot rather than be alone, she asks again. She says perhaps it has something to do with not wrestling so hard with the responsibility of wanting and finding God.

"What?" David asks.

"I said that lately I've been praying for things. I never do. I can thank the universe for my health and my love and the fact I live a gentle life but lately I've been asking for things. I think it's scaring the hell out of me. I want things, finally."

David listens and doesn't want to ask her what she's asking for. It'll only make him feel trapped. He's seen enough death to know he's not God. He doesn't have to answer her prayers. Let the other guy. The idiot she's going to the music with.

"What about you?" she asks. "What you been asking for?"

David is just now wishing the Feds would cut the damn phone off. It seems like 10 minutes have gone by. Where are they when he needs them? "I ask for everything baby. That's who I am."

The Feds click. "Saved by the bell," he says and they both get off the phone knowing it was too painful for him to think what it is he's asking for.

Her husband calls her up. He is going skiing on his way back from work. Saved by the bell—she has another 2 days to herself. What is this that she wants to be by herself all the time?

Her journal entries all have the same refrain. "I need more time alone."

Why does she believe she has to be alone? Maybe she thinks that is the only safe place. Or worse, she is not good for anyone. She was a child that not even a mother could love.

"I paid your IRS bill for you," she says. This is the niggardly kind of love she offers him.

"I booked us a room at Treasure Island," he mentions. He must feel guilty too.

"When do you have to be back at the job?" she asks. Meaning the one out of town.

"I told the guy I would call him and let him know. It depends on what you want to do."

"What I want to do?" What has she got to do with it? She knows he wants her to ask him to stay. He wants her to not like his being out of town. He wants her to commit to the marriage. Treat it like a marriage.

"We'll talk about it on the beach," he says.

"We will?"

"That's what you said," her husband answers. "That you want to talk about everything on the beach."

Already she feels guilty. She's read enough existential philosophy to know that guilt will assuredly lead her to make the wrong choices. She's guilty because she wants him eternally devoted to her in another state. When she's 80, she might ask him for a conventional marriage. And then again, she might not even then.

How is she going to convince him that this way, this way of visits with each other, is a perfect marriage?

David tells her about a post traumatic stress psychiatrist who took him out drinking and to a sex club. Before the trial.

"Maybe it was a test," he says, sipping his third coffee.

"It was," she replies. "No shrink takes you out drinking and to a sex club. It's not part of the treatment. Unless you are Anaïs Nin. Or my mother. She slept with her psychiatrist and he committed suicide."

"In that order?"

"I would think so, wouldn't you?"

David goes on to tell how the psychiatrist sat back and watched as David rallied the women at the sex club up close and had them dancing on the table. David himself of course had nothing to do with the women, but he was the ringleader, as he tells it, befriending the women, raising the stakes so the girls could make a lot of money. He invited the entire Japanese customer population to his private band of table dancers and encouraged all that spending.

Mira is listening to this tale of David as Goliath.

She finds the story vulgar. She would have turned away from his rallying at the sex club.

She trusts him more where he is now. Stripped of everything, unable to posture. Here he has some aspects of holiness, Sodom and Gomorrah dispensed with.

When her husband comes home, he tells her not to worry about the mistakes she makes in her work. He will take care of her. She is not alone in the world.

Her husband.

She runs her hands through his hair while he is on his phone and he shoves her away. She kisses his neck and he jerks his head to push her off.

To show her.

Her husband.

He loves her, he is saying, but he has his list of grievances. He has his rights.

"Why do you act like I'm a visitor when people come over here?" her husband has said at different times. "Why did you not take my name? Why do you stutter over the word husband? Why do you never tell anyone you're married? Why do you call me your boyfriend?"

"I do it somewhat," she'll say, smiling, "as a joke."

"Freud says there are no jokes."

"Freud says there are nothing but jokes." She isn't sure she's right when she says that but she throws it out anyway.

Deflection, everyone's favorite tool in an argument.

"I love you and we are a couple," he says. "You have to let yourself trust that. I get tired of constantly convincing you that a relationship is a good thing," her husband said, most understandably.

"I love you, too," she says, and she means it, she loves him extraordinarily but she doesn't know what one does when one loves. She doesn't know how to feel safe.

"You're loving," he says, "and fun," as if he is tallying a plus and minus file for himself.

She walks over and puts her arms around him and this time he lets her. "Don't worry," she says, "the right things will happen."

"What does that mean?" he asks.

"It's all going to be alright."

"If you so say so," he replies.

She looks at him. "You know what? Neither of us are so trusting."

She married him thinking she would eventually go back to being alone and maybe, just maybe, he doesn't know he unconsciously married her for the same reason.

Now that her father has been dead, Mira goes to visit her mother occasionally as some kind of homage to family. It is always an uncomfortable undertaking. For one thing, her mother doesn't look at her. This has been true since Mira was born. Her mother looks off at an imaginary movie camera. Her mother is not sure what Mira's name is. She calls Mira Penelope. No, my name is Mira. But you were called Penelope. No, I wasn't. Her mother does not know what age Mira is. Nor her birthday, nor does her mother call her on Christmas.

Mira never knows whether her mother thinks that it is the daughter's role—to mother the mother.

Her mother says, "I am a survivor." Of life, she means. "When will you meet a man who suits you?" her mother asks.

"I'm married."

"Oh yes I forgot. He doesn't suit you."

Mira feels the same way and this is profoundly uncomfortable. To agree with her isolated, heartless mother is profoundly uncomfortable.

"It's been cold, hasn't it?" her mother says bitingly.

"Yes." Mira despises talking about the weather. "How are you getting on with Alan?" Mira asks to change the subject. Alan is her mother's 70-year-old boyfriend. They slept together for 35 years while she and Alan were married to different people. Now, with wives and husbands dispensed with through divorce or death, they are together. Her mother is buying him a Mercedes, cashmere clothes, and taking him to Egypt. They have just returned from St Moritz.

"It's wonderful. We are very alike, Alan and I," her mother says to the movie camera.

"Oh? How?"

"We both can't love."

Is that an apology?

They are silent. What else is there to say? Her mother does not want to know any facts about her daughter. When Mira was born, her mother reportedly announced, "I don't want to be her mother," and left Mira with her father. When Mira was three and her father took her to visit her mother, her mother said, "I don't want you to think of me as your mother. Think of me as your friend."

But her mother lied to her. She didn't want to be friends.

She looks over at her mother whose face is turned away. However, Mira has to concede that her mother never contradicted herself.

It was true; she didn't want to be a mother. It is Mira who makes these visits because Mira wants to be a daughter.

However, these visits always purge her of this urge and she leaves feeling that she too must be a survivor. Of aloneness.

Mira says, "I have to go" and her mother doesn't get up to say goodbye. Her head turns further away.

Mira imagines her mother's thoughts. Why is my daughter so deaf? So willful? What does she want? Let me be free, her mother pleads to the devil in silence.

Mira walks out the door, defeated. Permission granted.

Mira begins to feel relief as she pulls her legs into the taxi and is amazed at how friendly the cab driver is. His interest in her starts to warm the ice wound. She even doesn't mind his commenting on how it's unseasonably cool out. By the time Mira arrives home, she is back to herself. A self that, yes, is not that normal, but one that is no longer smarting at the ice whip of her mother's eternal discarding of her.

"You can control nothing from here," David says.

Mira answers, "Listen you can control nothing out here either."

"That's not true," he responds.

Oh yes it is, she says to herself, and decides to pay attention to her husband.

She must remember to visit her husband out of town where he is working. That is whom she made herself responsible to. She must be careful of how her own head turns away.

"God," Mira tells her husband on the phone, "I may have to come stay with you in that one room on your construction site if my business fails. I never know if they'll like these damn articles I write."

"I would love if you came here."

"You would?"

"Yup. What did you do today?"

"I saw my mother."

"That's too bad."

"It was."

Her husband yawns to signal he's tired, that's it and then he says, "Who loves you?"

She giggles. "You mean you do."

"That's right."

"That's it?"

"That's it."

She feels secure as she puts down the phone.

That's all she has, at least on the being loved part. That's it. She's not complaining. It's better than when she started.

David's daughter, when she visits him, draws pictures and makes cutouts with the prison paper napkins. He likes the way she then sits on his lap and moves his head toward her if he happens to look elsewhere. "Pay attention to ME," she says.

David can see his ex-wife watching them. Sometimes David and his ex-wife get to talking about joint property that's now her sole property. He silently wonders if he'll get any of it back. This is not the time to bring it up. Sometimes they talk about relatives, all the reference points of fifteen years together.

Eventually they get to how hard it is for her to raise a child by herself. She hadn't planned on that although it wasn't like he was home much before, she says. "You know," he replies, just to have a little fun, "they say drug dealers spend more time with their children than most fathers. We're home during the day." He laughs. His ex-wife is not amused. She gets back to how hard it is for her. And as they get back there, to how hard it is for her, that's when he's reminded that his wife is like the guards. She wants him punished.

Mira asks her husband out to dinner. They go to the Japanese restaurant that has a special on. Before they go, Mira knows the special is a trick of some sort. Half price yakitori if you buy $40 of raw fish. Her husband is excited at the prospect of a bargain.

They order and Mira suddenly realizes she has nothing to say to him. Everything is dangerous. If she begins talking on anything, he will find a way to correlate it to her incessant independence, her lack of commitment to coupling. Finally her husband says, "If you were me, what would you do?"

"About what?"

"About us."

"You mean whether you should stay with a woman who won't have a child?"

"Yes."

She picks at her seaweed salad. "If you want a child," she says, "what I would do is get over me."

He nods. "I suppose you're right."

They are both exhausted with how this might be an impossibility. Not because she is so special but because, her husband, like herself and everyone else, longs for the longing.

David's brother said he was coming to visit in 2 days. This imminent visit has tired David before it even happens. Sometimes he just doesn't want to go through the energy of a visit. You feel you have to make the visit worthwhile for your visitor. Show you're still strong, hip. Ask about the plays you've read about in the New York Times. Ask your brother to send you a book you read about in the New York Review of Books. You have to show you're still a player.

It's work. Sometimes you're just too damn sad and tired and would just rather be alone. You don't want to strain that you are really free, even though you're not. And half the visitors seem like they're in prison themselves so they don't give you much of a hit. Beauty does, but it's fleeting. Look but don't touch. They take their beauty with them when they leave. Even the visits where you laugh a lot, it's great, you're laughing but you can already hear the lock down coming.

David smiles a lot and gesticulates during the visit with his brother. Swivels on his chair. Yes, this is a party if you want it to be.

But it's so goddamn short, finite, withheld, over. His brother will walk out and leave him here, confined.

Maybe why her husband doesn't smile when Mira and he visit with each other in the kitchen, or in the bedroom. Maybe her husband knows that it's so damn short, finite, withheld, over.

LETTERS

The only way they can unguardedly hold each other is to fondle letters. She recognizes his printed handwriting on the envelope at once, the way he underlines her name, the way his handwriting bursts out, shouting and separating itself from the bills and circulars his letters share her box with.

She sits down at her desk, opens his letter and settles down into his body of words.

Dear Mira,

A college philosophy professor of mine, a Dr. James Calwell, whom I admired greatly, said to me during one of our many rap sessions in the student cafeteria, "Human experience is a lifelong process of attempting to negotiate the inevitability of loss . . . and religion is a way to help wrestle with that loss . . ."

Upon reflection I can't imagine any religion or a combination of theologies that would ease the pain that the grip of not having you . . . would produce . . .

I just love being with you . . . looking at you . . . holding you . . . listening to you, . . . every blasted little thing about you . . .

Just a quick note to let you know what's going on in my head . . . and heart . . .

Much love, Theogenes

Theogenes, she smiles. What he calls himself. The gladiator prisoner tied to a rock and forced to fight to the death for the amusement of the Romans. He won an unheard of 110 fights. He died, finally, of exhaustion.

Mira folds the letter into her pocket, runs down the stairs surrounded by his silly words of love as she goes to see the seamstress. The words are hers, the present she just received, and she finds herself smiling at the people she passes on the street and smiling at the way they smile back at her.

There's a pile of letters on his cot but he has to see a guy about getting some spaghetti and you have to be in the mood to read letters anyway. He often rips them up without reading them at all. Why bother? They remind him too much that he's witnessing his own funeral. Everyone's life going on without him.

But before lights out (a misnomer, they never turn the lights out), after he has foraged some tuna and apples, he settles down on his cot, and opens one. Reluctantly.

Dear David,

I had to go interview for a job today at Stop and Shop. I hope I get it even though it doesn't pay much BUT I NEED THE MONEY. Elaine came over for dinner last night, I made pasta and crème caramel, your favorite. She's going through this thing with Brad. He wants to move to Vermont and she doesn't want to. I really hope I get this job. Oh I saw the Jane Tennyson thing on television I told you about. A British murder mystery. Everybody loves it.

I hate this cold and my car isn't starting properly. I don't have the money to fix it and taxes are coming up and I'm scared of those too. I hope you're doing okay. Everybody talks about you. Write me. Love Susan

Jesus who the fuck can handle the drivel.

Mira has sent a letter too. He doesn't want to have to put up with another letter that says nothing, even from her, so he skims Mira's for the parts about how she feels about him, for that will infuse his blood with some hope, courage, to go on. Is he primary to anyone out there?

Mira's letters don't sound as trapped as everyone else's but they're moody. Trouble with work usually. Sometimes they are exuberant, usually when her husband is out of town.

Dear David,

You should have been there (well you were actually, in my mind. I kept asking how you liked it.) I went to hear Pharaoh Sanders last night. The piano player and the percussion were amazing. Banging it out. It went on and on. True, pouring, all those insides, beating it out. After they finished, I was the one exhausted. So I went walking in the East Village to the drug-dealing street (5th) with $200 in my pocket, wearing my gold watch, and I asked myself, Why am I doing this? I finally figured out I was there to defy the odds. There to show that I could get away with it. That I wouldn't get caught. Then I came home and played music for Nancy who is staying with me while she is in town. Remember her? She's the one who works at a big press and you wanted her to publish books for children whose fathers are in prison. She is publishing books now about musicians in the 60s. But she's hardly heard of any of the musicians. What were you doing in the 60s, I asked her. Turns out she was in sororities while the rest of us were turning on with music. Or, like you, with war.

David stops here. He rereads the opening out loud to his celly. They begin rewriting the story with themselves as the protagonists. When they were on the Lower East Side. How they feel about Pharaoh Sanders. Rick never heard of him but he did go to hear Chet Baker in Frisco, unbelievably.

Pumped in energy. They are sick of the men's shouts, fuck yous and what the fuck man. These are ladylike preoccupations. Small, delicate. He and his celly get a hit of new conversation and then go back to talking about who left today and who's got how much time. David drops the letter by his cot after checking the envelope one more time for a money order.

Dear Mira,

You are fast becoming my blood bank in this world of hemophiliacs . . . I find myself coming to depend on you more and more . . . For some strange reason it makes me somehow responsible for you in some small way . . . and I like that . . . I must warn you that I have a bandage on my thumb the size of an orange . . . and a low grade fever . . . making me delirious . . . so I can't be held responsible (now there's a contradiction) . . .

(I usually put lines in like the last one when I am about to toss myself into a "parlous situation" as old wild Bill Shakespeare would say) . . . so what the hell should we call this one . . . words hot and sticky from the Dicky of DGB . . . the G stands for Gregarious . . . by the way . . . or how about . . . Fever pitch FUNK for Mira to junk, or hold in the cold of dismay . . .

Sitting in the middle of the rec-yard the other day . . . new set of batteries in my radio . . . slammin' reception . . . Copeland's

Appalachian Spring comes on . . . such a rich expansive sadness to the piece . . . makes my hair stand on end and gives me shivers . . . made me think of Martha Graham . . . and the dance she choreographed for the piece . . . magical . . . then read a biography of Copeland years later . . . and he stated that when he wrote the piece . . . he had not the least bit of a notion of relating or connecting to or impressing life in Appalachia . . . Anyway . . . get moving davyboy you only have an hour with this typewriter . . . and you only have nine fingers . . . or better yet . . . I think of myself as sort of like Sissy Hankshaw . . . that character on *Even Cowgirls Get the Blues*, the one with the huge thumbs . . . except I only have one . . . what was that great line in the book . . . by Delores Del Ruby . . . The enemy of women is not men . . . the enemy is the tyranny of the dull mind . . . Anyway . . . back to Copeland . . . *Appalachian Spring* . . . the piece reminds me of relationships . . . between two people that are close . . . in a way . . . with its sudden changes and melodic swings . . . intense . . . penetrating one moment . . . and quiet . . . listless the next . . . I imagined you there on the grass listening with me . . . I have become quite good at conjuring you up when the time is right . . . I rub the lamp . . . and GENIE MIRA appears . . . (this is obviously a private and convenient deception on my part) . . . it's a method of cushioning the undeniable longing . . . and what is this longing . . . this desire . . . this affection . . .

So I switch to other pressing thoughts . . .

I ponder this rage I read about for men's groups . . . Anybody interested in a sweat lodge should come inside here and they'll find out about being a man in a New York minute . . .

Gotta go.

I love you like quicksand.

Love,

Theogenes

Dear David,

I saw Vincent this weekend and he asked me if I knew your girlfriend, Susan? No, I said, I've never met her. Aha I can see you squirming. I always knew there was a Susan and probably a Maryann and an Elaine and a Babette as well. It's your right. You can't be forgotten.

Jesus, do you think I have the right to ask for fidelity? I'm not exactly out here being faithful myself.

Dear Mira,

Susan means nothing. You do.

Dear David,

"Truth is established by my capacity to convince you." Perelman is alleged to have said this. Do you think this quote would resonate with the counterfeiters and other new friends you're making in there?

Peter is sitting by the window in the kitchen, smoking. She is running a bath and calls out to him, just to share what she is thinking. If she shares what she is doing, she is not doing anything wrong. "David's letters are . . ." she says over the running bathwater. "Baudelairian rants, when you think about it. Performance art. He's like a dandy—unable to attach." She stops running the water. Peter is still smoking. "Pretty boys, they are, who overthrow the law for a good lay or a ten thousand dollar watch. Or for the joy of an aesthetic crime. De Quincey wrote an essay, 'Murder Considered as One of the Fine Art.' He was right on."

Peter doesn't reply and she wonders if her husband can make any sense of this or whether he's even listening. She has made the assumption, with that doggedness of all writers, that what she is thinking about is interesting to everyone. "I wonder if that essay is in the prison library," she continues.

"I don't know why you think about it so much," from him.

Considered as a Fine Art, she says to herself.

"Who knows?" she replies.

He moves to the television and she leaves the now waiting bathtub and follows him and kisses his head as he flicks to the McNeil Lehrer report but before she returns to the bath, she goes to her desk and skims David's letter once more for a requisite connection to her.

Then she carries the letter into the living room where Peter is lying down. She waits for the commercial. She at least does that.

"You see," she says when she thinks he might be interested, "you can tell from his letters this is not a man used to talking to people without an angle. He finds an angle for his letters. An aesthetic that precludes moral decision. He will get what he can get. Want to hear some?"

"No, I don't."

"Alright."

She stares at the television but nothing registers. So she kisses Peter lightly on the lips (what a risk. David has helped) and sashays into the bathroom, to the tub, telling herself that David's shorter notes are the ones she likes best, those that are rushed out of his cell as missives, investment deposits in the bank of keeping him forefront.

Peter suddenly appears in the kitchen to fill his glass with Orangina. The kitchen is next to the bathroom so she can see him from her tub.

"You know what else?" she says. "All those guys in prison take on different personas out of boredom. They reinvent themselves. They change personas as they change prisons. They tell each other they know Boesky, Kennedy, Kissinger. Put on British Upper class accents. Or Cockney accents that they think are Upper class."

"Why do you find this so interesting?"

"It's a microcosm."

"No, it isn't." He turns away to go back to MacNeil Lehrer and she notes he is carrying a book.

"What's that?" she asks.

"A book on wooden shipbuilding."

"Are you going to make a wooden boat?"

He stops before going back to the TV in the living room. For once, he sounds a bit chatty. "Maybe. But a motor is $2000. You have to maintain it. There are a lot of complications. But I might build one."

"Oh."

"So many things to build," he says. "That's how I keep sane."

"You're sane?" she asks, teasing.

"A lot more than he is."

"Probably," she answers.

Then he says, "Have a good bath," and leaves for the couch and world news. So much easier to handle than dealing with an eccentrically minded wife.

"I'll be out in a second," she calls out. She wants to be with him, she does want to be close.

No answer.

He probably could care less, she thinks.

He is gone and all is emotionally still and she decides that she and her husband are really very much alike. Neither of them puts much faith in the other.

Dear Mira,

Been reading for the last 10 minutes but knowing nothing of what I've read because I was lost in thoughts of you. I was thinking about what you said . . . I'm going to go with my feelings right now, . . . which brought you to mind . . . a line or two from Ulysses . . . This vegetable world is but a shadow . . . hold to the now . . . the here . . . through which all future plunges to the past . . .

Also thinking about my passion for you . . . of which there is a tremendous tenderness . . . not disarming it by any means, . . . but coupled with it . . . making it hotter . . .

There are times when I can feel you running through my veins . . . and I feel so close to you . . .

God, he can go on and on. He must have the time.

How could he risk prison over love anyway? she wonders. Why would he go on such a solitary journey? Why didn't he stay with his wife? Work out the mundaneness of marriage, the mundaneness of a living, rather than get himself sent to jail?

Does he write about love rather than living it? Or did he believe in such an abundance that he could take a rest for awhile?

Her husband says, "He deserves to be punished. He was breaking the law."

"Well you yourself were one of his customers. You bought marijuana from one of his lackeys. That's a little hypocritical of you."

Peter doesn't reply to that. Then he asks, "Are you in love with him?"

"Of course not. He's crazy. But I like his madness. It interests me."

"Well watch out. He's serious, while you're doing social research. He's going to want to connect. He's going to show up. And I'm not going to let him in here. So get that straight."

"No womanizer goes for a woman who's lost her looks."

Peter doesn't reply.

Does that mean he agrees, she wonders.

"I got a letter from David. Want to hear it?"

"Why would I want to hear what a con has to say? Can't you see? I've heard enough."

"Don't be angry," she says, going over to the couch and putting her arms around him. She really does love Peter, she thinks. They have been through so much together, just trying to be loving. "You know the guy saw a lot of action and it affected him. Be compassionate."

Peter says, "You saw a lot of action too. Only much younger."

She laughs. "Sometimes," she says, "you are so right on."

He smiles proudly. Finally, finally, she's seeing him.

Dear David,

Just went and had my face cleaned. The woman who gives the facial described her husband in exactly the same terms as I describe mine. Doesn't brush his teeth every day. Forgets to eat. Goes to the doctor when pushed and tells the doctor how to diagnose him. Do you think we're married to the same man?

But what I'm writing about is will you be there next Wednesday?

If so, I'm coming. If you've escaped, leave me a voice message.

Gotta go. My hair is wet and people are coming for the weekend and I still have some articles to write. I just want to set up a date.

All broads are crazy he decides. He hopes she shows Wednesday because he hates when she says she will and then she doesn't. Hates it.

Mira walks into the living room and her husband waves he is busy. He is reading the Want Ads for a motor for his boat. He does not want to be disturbed.

David has decided to give Mira the silent treatment. He'll write her but no phone calls. Her husband seems to have won her with alleged limited communication. And anyway why the hell did she get married anyway? No, he is not going to be toyed with. Not him.

Everyone knows nothing rouses a woman's interest more than being ignored. You win women by giving them buckets of attention or pretending you only slightly notice them. Till you're married. Then you give them a little of both or a combination, the middle ground as his ex-wife would talk endlessly about. Anyway he's going to stop calling her for a while.

He has to admit Will's got that Kansas horse sense. Probably what made him rich as an oil trader.

When he told Will he was going to stop calling Mira so as to double up her interest in him, Will said, "Daaaaavid my man, that's good. Except not calling her is also going to arouse your interest in her."

"No man, I can shut them out," David said. "You don't know me."

"Shut them out? While you're painting them up there in the art room?"

"Yup. Shut them out," David said, "and you get back your power."

"That's a helluva way to love someone, Daave. No wonder you ended up in jail."

She waits for Peter to come home. As she waits, she reads the New York Review of Books. He still hasn't come home so she begins reading the personal ads. Darcy looking for Elizabeth Barrett Browning. Heloise and Abelard. All these people wanting to fall in love through letters. The Times has an article about a man suing his wife for divorce because she was unfaithful on e-mail. All these people writing out their love.

So many people died through a letter not delivered in time.

David's last letter is on top of her pile of papers, medicine cards, checkbook, Kleenex, stapler, his letter, but who can pay attention to that monkey business right now.

However, she glances down at it.

"Mira . . .

. . . about midnight . . . and I must hurry if I'm to get this to post in time . . . just wanted to bounce a few thoughts off you . . .

Bach's birthday Monday . . . great stuff on the radio . . . he was rejected in his time, . . . relegated to the 3rd or 4th string . . . do you believe it . . .

I've been thinking lately . . . and I don't mean to preach . . . It's important to be who you are, . . . who you want to be . . . no one has worn more fucking hats than yours truly . . . and it's a sad waste of time . . . you've been held down . . . not respected, not appreciated for who you are . . . so you haven't been happy that's why you haven't felt good about yourself, . . . it takes a lot more than perseverance to live . . . it takes intent . . . a driving desire to trust . . .

I don't mean to sound preachy . . . I just don't want to see a beautiful flower penned in, . . . when she should be allowed to bloom wild . . .

Love you unconditionally,

Theogenes

Figures he would oh so lightly promise her love for her real self. Cons are supposed to know your weakness before you do.

As if she is remotely a flower. That's her weakness. She doesn't know who she is, she decides.

Figures he would serenade her. But what does the music mean?

Mira begins to answer him while she's waiting for her husband to come home. It's with her husband she has to face the uphill climb towards surrender, towards safety and love.

She must hold to that. These are letters.

MADNESS

David waited three weeks to see the prison dentist who comes once a month. God forbid your teeth are knocked out and all the nerves are screaming bloody murder. You'd have to go to one of the inside drug dealers or do a plumbing job of your own.

The dentist is a young black woman, whose white coat is as crisp as some of the men keep their uniforms. She has soft dark brown eyes and bad skin. She sits David down in an old school desk chair and pulls out the pick and mirror and David begins his woman thing with his fast mind, ocean blue eyes and pretty smiles that it's not long before the fat dental assistant whose hair is slicked back tight to her head says cheerfully in Spanish, Let's take this one home.

Ah he still has it. Which is amazing considering how the center does not hold. He got a card from an old buddy who said that God was with him and that Jesus had died on the cross for David's sins. That David was not alone, there was God's love.

This guy always seemed normal to Dave.

Not to mention, Mira is beginning to sound like St Theresa of Avila herself. Says she has taken the vow of quiet and internal nursing. All she wants is time alone. Well, she's getting it. No calls from him, oh no. He doesn't like those Spanish phrases she's started ending phone calls with. Te quiero mucho. Te adoro. He knows where the fuck she's been learning those. He tells her that the art room teacher is Puerto Rican, a woman built like a solid square. David says, You've got your Puerto Rican and I've got mine. Because David is sure she's having croissants and coffees with some Nuyorican. Well the whole world is Spanish; let's face it. When he gets out and dreams of prison, his dreams will be in Spanish. Mira said a Puerto Rican guy was trying to pick her up at the gym and while he was busy showing her how to lift her legs (a thought David did not find entertaining, is she stupid or what), she found out he was a screw at Sing Sing.

I can't get away from your story is what she said to David.

Well, I can't get away from it either.

Enough of her. Enough of everybody. He is so fucking fed up with it here. He remembers that people used to say that nothing was worse than incarceration and listen it is bad but you can survive it like those two little girls in *Life Magazine* who have only one body and they think they're having a helluva time. You can survive anything but it's so damn boring and petty and repetitive and infuriating and you do those damn weights and sit ups so as not to fucking kill someone. Even on the phone. His lawyer has been ditzing around. He knows the deal better than his lawyer does. He knows the cases that have worked. The guys and he talk more law than they do at Harvard Law School. Action is what he wants. Action.

His life is trying to quiet himself down, put a lid on his franticness. Sedate it. Hold on.

Someone suggested he join a Veteran's group in here. He went, it's not like he's too busy to go, and all these saps sitting in a circle sorry about what happened over there but he isn't so why should he sit around with these guys pussying about the hurt of seeing their buddies legs and heads blown off? It was their finest hour, who are they kidding, to be tested like that. They lived parts of themselves they'll never live again. They learned something. He learned something. What are they crying about?

There is no order to this world, none at all. Everybody in groups or marriages or professions or self help programs trying to create order, find a way to dam up thinking and have a language to replace living. Jesus. It's pathetic.

You come in alone, you go out alone. All these people out there running around making friends and communicating about this and that and doing a favor here and a favor there, all these people feigning interest in another's life so as to get a break from their own—what is this shit? It's not being who you are. Okay, okay we need people, sure, but not as much as we tell ourselves. It is not only the hurt animals who go off alone. It's the courageous ones, the scouts, like Nietzsche and Beethoven, who go off alone, dismantle everything and build it up anew. It's lonely, will drive you crazy but Jesus what else is there? You hang around too much with these milk minds, pretty soon you're thinking in milk.

He goes down to Ildefonso's cell and lately even this Puerto Rican has been getting on his nerves. Ildefonso is getting depressed so he never agrees to anything. Want to come down for dinner? No, I'm not hungry. Want to come up and see the guys' paintings? No. Nothing. Ildefonso is always in a bad mood. His son is being arraigned, might even be joining him in here. But that's not what's getting Ildefonso down. What's getting him down is he doesn't have control of his life.

David is tired of all of them. He's glad Ildefonso's saying No. He even hopes Will is depressed and hanging in his cell because right now everybody pisses him off. There's not enough strong energy in here. Everyone is weak. Pussy footing round the fucking guards. He can forget himself painting and he does but sometimes even that is hard. He doesn't have the energy; the anger is worked out of him. People walking close to the walls.

This is nowhere. Lately in this jail they don't even send you to the hole. He can't even get frothed there. It's just one little day after the other with its little regimens. Food, waiting in line, beefed up conversations, art classes, and reading. Mira says, Doesn't sound bad to me. Let her try it. He's read everything in the prison library. From crossing the Arctic to how to take apart a turbocompressor. Everything.

His ex-wife doesn't even send goddamn magazines. Mira doesn't order a book he asked for. So what if it's a little difficult to find. If a friend of his was in prison, he'd do everything to keep them going. Send stuff. Work on getting them out. But everybody he knows just accepts the goddamn thing, like it's a point of interest, like he's gone away to college or something. There's not a person he knows who has not smoked marijuana and yet he is supposed to go away for them, like Jesus Christ. He gets to do all the years locked up and everyone puffing away.

The tediousness is what it is. Plain tediousness of living. Even though he's made a vow not to call anyone, he has to. It's just too tedious. Like everything is, at that 5.00 hour when there are no cocktails, no dinner or romance plans. Tedious.

So he walks over to the phone, and the hell with his dialectics, he dials Mira's number collect. She's not home of course. It is a Friday night when normal people are making plans. Cooking or booking dinner. Changing clothes. Leaving one reality for another and he can't. That's the drill.

But it did feel better dialing the number. Even if he does believe we should all go it alone. It's absolutely fucking impossible.

Peter's just told himself he's not going to call his damn wife up. Other wives would be making dinner right now for their husband or planning a pleasant evening, but no doubt his wife is staring out the window or in the bathtub reading a book, insistent on the city. He's still out of town, his business requires him to build in his hometown, and he knows he could make a plan to see her but why bother? She won't pay attention to him in a way that feeds him. Where her mind is focused on pleasing him.

So instead he goes to the local library and takes out some books on wooden shipbuilding. He's going to build himself a wooden boat.

He knows not calling will upset her. She'll start vividly imagining another woman or that he doesn't love her. She'll read into it and it'll make her nervous and if she breaks down and calls him, her voice will have a slight quaver to it. She will even be a little appeasing, groveling. She might even say she's considering moving to his house.

He knows it upsets her when he pulls away but she has got to realize how she gives him nothing.

He used to dream of taking Mira away with him on a boat. Or he would dream of he and Mira all alone in his house, she happy upstairs, doing her dreaming or reading and he working downstairs in the cellar.

Isolation like that? she said. It's neurotic.

Mira's capable of spending about 8 minutes alone with him and then she's nervously looking around for a book, for a phone, or at his face for some message.

He dials Lee Nattie whose house he has agreed to work on tomorrow. It's Saturday but Peter likes to work.

Mira asked him if he would like to do something next weekend, Easter, and he told her he would think about it sometime when he wasn't working.

Saturday morning, he gets in the car and drives by the seashore to visit Geof Richon, another contractor on his way to Nattie's. Geof invites him and gives him a beer. Geof is on his third wife who happens to be sitting there, a younger woman who has a bit of a headache. They ask Peter where his wife is. He says she's in the city. They're working a few things out.

"Who isn't?" Geof says.

Peter doesn't want to admit that his wife won't get pregnant but he alludes to it. Geof says, "That's tough." Geof says this new wife (who has gone upstairs) is going to want a child and he's already got two of his own, already grown.

"Your wife will win," he tells Geof.

Geof agrees. But Peter can't win because he hasn't got that power. He tries to impregnate Mira when they're having sex. He wills it. Even when she turns her head away. She's stopped having orgasms as if that stops pregnancy. They both know it's a power struggle. He sneers when she goes into the bathroom to put in birth control. He tries to make her as uncomfortable as possible.

Why would she not want a kid? She says that money is an issue.

Peter took her to a shrink and said, "What kind of woman worries about money when having a child?"

The shrink said, "Every woman."

Mira smiled, victoriously.

Yes, they live week to week and yes he is a carpenter but they could make it. They could move to his house over the sea and live in a small town. Her eyes glaze over when he says that.

What is she so busy doing?

Geof says, "I respect something about Mira, though. She seems to be herself."

Peter nods.

They get onto an easier subject like getting the ordinances from the state to change the school into low income housing and then Peter says he's got to go over to Lee's and thanks Geof for the beer and walks out the pathway to his old Volvo.

Lee needs a new roof and because Lee is in a wheelchair from a car crash, he has asked Peter to take care of it.

Lee obviously doesn't have any kids and he accepts it. But then Lee has had to accept a lot. But then so has Peter. He was an orphan and now she wants to make him childless. Another lost family. Well the hell with her he thinks carrying some tar paper through Lee's garden.

He works hard for 5 hours straight, stripping off the shingles, putting the tar paper down. He only breaks to smoke camels. He exhausts himself. This is something his wife always admired about him. That passion. Why doesn't she realize he could love her with the same passion? There's a chill in the air and he likes the briskness. He likes fighting the elements. His whole life has been that.

At 2 he goes over to the sauna. Strips down with all the other men and they sit in that hot little building and talk recent real estate and wife changes. The owner of the sauna asks him where Mira is. "That's some wife you got there. A pretty girl."

"She's okay. She's in the city working as usual."

"Smart kid."

He smiles to the men like everything is okay, not like the fact he hardly sees his wife and when he does he's angry at her elusiveness so he leaves the hot house naked and runs to the cold water quarry and jumps in. He yells as he hits the water. He forgets everything in the cold water, forgets his hot rage at how so many many people let him down.

He comes out of the water and goes back into the sauna and the older men are talking about the police notes in the local news, sons and grandsons of friends who have chosen to become petty criminals. Seems to be the new career growth opportunity. The guys pat him on the back for his courage facing the icy quarry and tell him they'll see him next week.

He fires up the car and goes back to Lee's. The sun is weak but he finishes laying down the tarpaper and covers it in case it rains and walks into Lee's and tells him he'll see him next Saturday to finish the job off. It should hold for the week though.

Lee is sitting in his chair reading, listening to Herbie Hancock. Peter thinks a single male life like this would not be that bad. All this willing to get your wife to do what you want. People have told him that will get him nowhere but if he doesn't push hard with a renegade wife like his, he'll get nothing. He has to wear her down.

On his way to his room in his house, he picks up a paper, gets some orange juice, ham and cheese, and swings by Larry Dahlmer's the boat builder who for some odd reason calls him Boy. Larry thinks this wooden boat building idea of his is impractical. Larry focuses on all the problems of building a boat since that's his business and it's been fraught with problems but this boat building that Peter wants to do, Peter explains to Larry, would be for pleasure. He likes to be doing something.

He wasn't always like that but she has taught him that. Mira doesn't even sit in the dentist's chair without reading a book. And if she puts her book down, she studies her own x-rays as the dentist checks her teeth. The dentist told him. Somehow that part of her has rubbed off on him. He doesn't want to fall into depression and he knows he could. No one likes to feel alone and he is alone. She is not here and never has been.

Peter takes a rowboat out to the boat Larry lives on but Larry is not there so he rows back, docks the boat at George's Low Tide Marina.

Peter gets into his old Volvo, and drives to his house. He climbs the granite stairs and walkway that he built with his own hands. He settles in and makes himself a sandwich, checks the machine and notices she has had the wherewithal not to call. He can imagine it hurt her; she gets nervous without his contact. She needs to know he is there. He sits down at his chair and opens one of his books and bites on the sandwich. She's decided to live a nun's life and has turned his into a monk's. Women, always setting the tone. When is he supposed to?

He's waiting for something bad to happen. That's what he told her when she asked what was going to happen. "Something bad," he said.

"Like what?" she asked, appalled. "Like I die?" Although she assumed he meant that one of them fall for someone else.

"No," he said.

"Like one of us falls for someone else?"

"No," he said.

He was just threatening her.

That's the life force he's living now. And understandably, he's tired.

Mira has a coffee in the morning, and listens to one of Beethoven's *Bagatelles*. She thinks this might be the music they play as you enter Heaven. She answers a letter from a woman who bores her but who tells her that her marriage seems to thrive on separations. As if she and her husband could make that their form.

Last night Mira went out swing dancing. She didn't know the steps but she twirled and sweat to the big bands, while men older than she told her to one two one two back at high speed, and on the slow dances pulled her too close to their aging stomachs. But it was the twirling and the not talking to any of the men she enjoyed. The changing partners with no responsibility.

She loved that. She did not want to even know their names. She liked their reaching their hands out for her to join them for a dizzy fast dance and then throwing her off for a spin. She liked the quick thank you when the music ended and the way the men went off to roam for another woman to twirl around them and how she sat down to rest and if one came, fine, if not, fine. She loved that freedom.

Her legs were tired as she walked home from the Continental Club. Her machine had one message but she knew it wasn't her husband. She didn't even play it. She knew she was being punished. He was returning next week. They would fall back into their habitual snuggling and silence. They would begin renting movies and she would return to picking food off his plate at the neighborhood restaurants.

She liked the walking next to him. She liked his voice. Maybe even she liked his distance.

As she waited for her husband's return, or for anyone's return, but a return to her nonetheless, if it ever happens that someone returns to her, she had walked in the weak Spring sun. She had been like a child hurrying toward the patches of sunlight as if it is was a game to jump into the light, warmer spaces along her walk.

The night before at a friend's birthday dinner, the women had sat away from her. For what? For her oddness.

Why did they sit away from her? She was older than they, in many ways less accomplished. She had had no education, no parents to cook her a meal, to pay her bills. She had no phone calls showing parental interest in her. On Christmas, Easter and her birthday, she never heard from anyone, except her husband. She had been borne and then told to make do.

All those wives with their degrees and their long legs had shunned Mira.

Did they think they would catch the disease of a husband who goes away and might leave you forever? A husband who is angry at you? Did these women think they would catch the disease of lovelessness?

A musician at the dinner part had to leave early and so Mira begged off to go with him, so she wouldn't be alone on the subway, left him at his stop, and only when she got into bed did she realize she had not said goodbye to anyone.

The women's rejection. Like her mother's. What off keynote did Mira continually play? The women left her to sit with men who were obligatorily kind, like big dogs. How's it going with you and your husband, Mira? Oh, that's good. It'll work out. Don't think about it.

Like her mother had left her to her father. It'll work out.

Mira had not had the strength to walk over to the women. Not had the strength to ask for their kindness. Paralyzed by the emotions of her past.

Home now, with her books and Beethoven and the buses going by and the dogs she recognized on the street. Home, her home. Everything of her husband's in place. All that was missing was him and even his not being there made little difference.

Oh, she knew, she knew she didn't have the courage for love. Nor the artistry for lies. She was in no woman's land.

Losing her beauty. What use had it been? Always got you a job, always got you the possibility of a stranger. She would give a smile and get a smile. No cosmetics can shield her coming effacement. She could not afford tucks and anyway she wondered how much difference they made. The retreating from the center stage of the sexual theater went on inside too. She was at the age where younger people didn't have much hope for her. And worse, she was not sure what hope she had for herself.

Forty-five. And working at half attention, married at half attention. Forty-five and still sustained by the amusement of a new lipstick color or hearing a new piece of music. Forty-five and it is still the sun and warm baths that heal her. The ocean surrounding her. Forty-five and still unable to be as original as she had hoped. Still excavating inner truths and still they come out garbled. Forty-five and still, maybe, the four year old who had been happy her mother left but seared that she had not been a soul worth staying for. Forty-five and still she entered a room, sure of only one thing, she might not be worth staying for. Know me and you will be disappointed. Forty-five and a husband who clung to his tangible home and wanted a tangible wife. And here Mira cannot make her hands hold the tangible. Everything sieves through.

TRUE LOVE

"Let's have dinner out," Mira says. "I have to talk to you."

Her husband has been back in town only a week. A week in which they settled back into their frightened friendship. They were polite and solicitous of each other, broken only occasionally by a vicious impatience with the other.

He busied himself going to the dentist, picking up tools at his shop, and looking at jobs. She worked, saw friends, went to plays and took long walks with mystery characters. She also saw the doctor.

The red, green and white Christmas lights make the restaurant she picks (not the usual diner, let's have a bit of gentility for this upcoming news) seem festive on this hot summer night.

"Listen," she says to her husband's menu behind which he is sitting, "Remember how I said I had something to talk about. Well, this is weird what I'm about to tell you. I'm pregnant."

The menu comes down. He is trying to stifle a smile into a blank face.

He does this so she won't get scared. He knows that if he pushes in any way now, she'll take the opposite tack. She is an outlaw in love. This is what he has to deal with.

She says, "Don't get too happy. I don't know what I'm going to do yet."

Of course, Mira doesn't play these scenes like the Hallmark commercials, he's thinking. She wouldn't fall into his arms saying, I'm so happy. I want to have your baby. She's figuring out how to get rid of it. That's her habit. She had two abortions with him when he first met her. But then he didn't want the children either, although he makes a point of never admitting that. He looks at her sitting across from him, she does look healthy, very healthy, hair shining, skin glowing, healthy, but he catches that she occasionally bites her lip.

He has to be careful how he responds. She's against family, against unity. The happiest he's ever seen her is when she drives the car too fast.

However, she's his now.

He gives his order to the waiter in a deeper voice than usual. He's a man. He just got his middle-aged, almost menopausal wife pregnant. Just like that. Didn't even have to try. Just made her feel guilty enough, scared her about using the birth control. In fact, when you think about it, he made his middle-aged wife young. It takes a real man.

"I'm not sure what I want to do," she says again. "I never wanted a child." Don't you see, I am a child? "I'm going to think hard about it for the next 3 weeks. We can talk about it."

"Okay," he says as the waiter sets down his calamari. He reaches for the ketchup.

She goes onto various one sided debates over dinner about their poverty stricken financial situation since he is a carpenter, a good one, but this is New York, let's face it, Wall Streeters feel poor here, then she rants on about their legendary insecurity as a couple, their indomitable incompatibility, she even has the nerve to throw that in, but he isn't listening too hard. She frequently goes on these lecture series that tire even her. The trick is not to respond. The next morning she'll kiss him over coffee as if they were out of *A Man and a Woman*.

As far as he's concerned, he's won.

She had plans to see David before she found out this latest dire news. She's still going. This is truth and everyone must know it. Anyway, she doesn't want to act any differently.

David smiles gaily as he enters the visiting room. You don't know what is about to hit you, she thinks. His blue eyes flash round the room, cornfields with flecks of gun chrome. The room gets lighter.

"Let's go shopping," she says.

"God you're going to be impossible on the outside."

She takes his hand and leads him to the vending machines. She puts her arms round his waist, taking in the whole mass of him, "God your body is so hard," she says.

"It should be, I work out about 19 hours a day." She runs her hands over his body to actually know this kind of hardness, never again will she, and then pulls her hands quickly back to herself. She doesn't want the guards over here. The apologetic guards. Hey man, we understand but you know . . . regulations . . . We don't want to interrupt you with your wife, they say.

He always likes it when they refer to her as his wife. She likes it too.

She pushes the vending machine buttons for popcorn. He gets spaghetti with meatballs. French fries. She hands him the money so he can break the rules of prisoners not holding currency. A cheap thrill to empower, free him.

He gets a coke, she gets a coffee. They heat the food in the microwave. She runs her hands up and down the stiff khaki material of his back as they wait for the microwave scream of completion. He pulls the food out of the microwave and then he is busy, getting ketchup, mustard, forks. Busy like he is working a recording studio.

She takes her food and walks to a locked down chair. He follows her with his hands full.

She places her food between them.

"What are you doing?" he asks and she moves her food onto her lap so they can be nearer each other.

She ends up, despite being pregnant, kissing his neck. What else is there to do in prison? She burrows her nose in the side of his face. You have to do something.

She takes in his smell, puts her arms round his pumped up shoulders. She has to stretch across.

"I have something to tell you," she says.

"Shoot."

"No, later, after we eat," she says. "When there's only one hour left."

About two hours before she is scheduled to leave, he says, "There's only one hour left."

"Okay, well, actually, what it is, is . . . I'm pregnant. I thought I was too old. I'm 45 for chrissake. I hardly even see him—"

"Is it his?" he asks.

"Of course," she says.

She sees David suddenly stand up. He towers over her, but seems unsteady. He is getting his balance standing up. She knows what he is thinking. Pregnant. Party over. She belongs to another man. Another thing taken away. She belongs to another man. She is going away. He is not looking at her. Avoiding her. Another thing he is stripped of. Even the fantasies of her are about to be taken away.

Then he abruptly sits down. She starts in, how she is trying to decide what to do, but he isn't listening.

"Follow your heart," he interrupts her.

She looks up at him as if he has just spoken another language. "Follow your heart," he says again.

That must be a stock line, she tells herself. Those words came too fast.

Then he asks her, "What do you want from me?"

Meaning: Why did you tell me?

"Nothing," she says.

Why'd she tell him, they both ask themselves.

She must want his love, she guesses. She wants to believe they can surmount her marriage, his record, her pregnancy, his girlfriends, her aging, her abortion, his being in jail, her inability to trust her feelings, her inability to trust him, their inability to trust themselves. She wants to feel they can surmount their improbability, her husband's and her own. Tell me we can surmount that.

She wants him to make it better.

Obviously, she can't.

Yes, she is excited she is pregnant. All her friends trying so hard to get pregnant and here she is fertile enough to get pregnant on a breath of love, not the work of it.

She is fecund, female.

But how can she have a baby with one man when she is thinking of another man?

This baby would make her honest.

"Follow your heart," he says. Neither of them can concentrate the rest of the visit. He walks her to the locked in door.

"Pick up some rattles on the drive home," he tells her.

In response, she punches his stomach lightly.

"If you abort, it's going to devastate your husband," he says to her.

She swallows. "That's obvious."

Even David thinks so and he's a person who never cared about devastating anyone's husband.

She looks up at him as she's saying goodbye, she blurts out that it could be his fault she's pregnant.

"It's your white heat. You enflamed me and made me vulnerable. I got excited by you and it made me more receptive."

He nods.

"Could be," he says.

He tells her a story about a mistress who got pregnant by him after trying for 10 years with her husband. David was married while with this mistress. The mistress aborted.

These stories frighten her. Everyone cheating and lying.

"Were you nice to her during the abortion?"

"I went with her," he says.

"Did you love her?"

"It was a sexual thing. She was very pretty."

"Well would you have left your wife for her?" Mira asks.

"No," he answers, "I wouldn't have left my wife for her."

She looks up at him and takes this in very slowly. She adds this new revelation to his criminal record.

When her husband comes home, she dutifully goes to the door and hugs him. "Scoop," she says in a low voice, smiling, as if she is happy to see him. But if she was really happy with him, she wouldn't have felt the need to go to the door and parody this dutiful wife.

She wouldn't be pushing it. It would just be. Alive, there between them.

The minute she takes in his tired face, his angular body that always holds himself away from her, she is disappointed. She can't spend the rest of her life with him. They don't meld together. His psyche is hard as rock. He tries to kiss her and she pulls slightly away. "Don't be frightened to kiss me," he says.

She brings him a beer and he sits down at the dining room table and takes off his shoes and socks. His feet smell. He says it was all day driving in wool socks.

Her feet don't smell and she did a lot of driving today herself. She keeps silent with this piece of fastidious information.

They talk of how he doesn't like his work, of his relatives who don't like their work; of the Cuban quarter in Tampa which Joe told him about and which her husband wants to see.

She feels weighed down. Nothing lights up on her interior switchboard as he speaks.

She is curled up on the black chair near the dining room table and suddenly knows that she does not love him in the right way. She likes him in the right way. She likes him alright, a decent hardworking lovely man. But she does not love him enough. He does not hold his flashlight high enough in their tunnel.

She looks at her watch and it is only 9 pm. She wishes they could just go to bed now and sleep.

Her phone rings.

"You must be planning on having it," David says. "Why else would you tell me? If I was visiting you in prison and was having an abortion, I wouldn't tell you."

Aha, she thinks, there's the difference. He wouldn't tell me.

"No," she says, "No. I want you to know all of me. I want you to know everything. What else have we got to give each other here, except the showing of ourselves?"

But truth is she told him to find out where he stands. This would be the proper time for him to tell her he loves his ex-wife; he's playing her, let her go.

He doesn't say any of that. He says she must follow her heart.

It's almost too much for her to hear. The future, what it's holding.

How could she lay this on him? David asks himself as he kicks the 1950s clothes dryer. He finally got it working. He can make anything work. He has a reputation for that in here. So the guys are going to be a little surprised when he says how he didn't make this work. That it broke for good. Broken. He's no longer needed in action. A goner. History. An extra in the movie. Niente. Over and out.

He tried to rob her from her husband and now he got robbed.

He continues on in his head as he folds his fucking underwear. Big excitement here today. All she was doing is telling me

I'm no one. All she's doing is telling me she may go away. Why else would she tell me?

Because it's over. And I can't fucking do anything about it.

Fuck the dryer. He'd like to punch someone.

"How the hell," her husband yells, "can you make a decision? You don't trust anything. You look at the dark side of things. It will all work out. If you act out of fear, you're going to regret this."

"Daave," Will says, "she must be going to have it." Will puffs and on his cigar on the Bleachers of Truth. "You've gotta face this. Why would she tell you?"

"I know."

Clarke who is getting out in 64 days is listening. Clarke is only 17 years old and in for growing marijuana, like Daave is, but his wasn't a million dollar business. A few plants, and even then he got 5 years. Clarke has decided to go back to this punishing horticultural career when he gets out.

"What a fool you are Clarke," Will says.

Clarke smiles prettily. He's got plenty of time. He's not old like these guys in their 40s. He's got plenty of time to lose or gain. He doesn't want to go straight. Not this young.

"This is not a place I want to come back to," Will says.

"You won't have to," Dave says. "With the way your appeal is going you'll be in here till you're 87."

"Now we're going to win this," Will says. "I'm getting Milken's lawyer in here. At least I'm not becoming somebody's step daddy. I don't have these problems, Daave."

"Jesus."

"You're just going to have to take the whole caboodle, Daave. She and her kids, all those kids she's going to have while you're in here enjoying yourself. You'll get out and can start helping her change diapers and heat formulas. Stay up all night. Ready for that, Daaave?"

"I'm ready for anything."

"Hell, I know that. But you are ready for THAT?"

"Yeah, I'm ready. What other choice have I got?"

"You can skedaddle Daave. Things look bad to me. If she aborts, you're going to owe her. If she doesn't, you can kiss her goodbye."

"I don't mind owing her Will. I don't look at it like you do. I dig her."

"Daave, things don't look the same in here as they do out there. We're desperate men. We're vulnerable. In fact when I get out I'm going to visit myself some women in prison. I'm about ready to meet some desperate women myself."

"Jesus, Will, sometimes you don't know what the fuck is going on."

"I'm not alone, Daave, not alone at all."

Her husband has the newspaper out in the coffeeshop. But he finds himself talking to the old guy from Maine who's sitting next to him. Her husband says, "My wife and I are going off to Florida in a month." The old guy and he are reading the national weather.

"Been cold down theyah."

"Picking up now," Peter says.

"My granddaughter is in a soccer camp down theyah," the old Mainer says. "She's a big girl. Five eleven."

"Are there professional girl soccer teams?"

"Nope. I don't think so. You got any kids."

Peter thinks a moment. He would love to tell this old guy that he's pregnant with one, he and his wife. That he's a normal guy with a normal path in front of him. About to begin his lineage but he is frightened of Mira's actions. She could make him a fool. Give him all this hope and then fuck it. She is almost surely going to let him down. Mira doesn't believe in life. "Nope, I don't have any kids. Not yet."

The old guy nods and, like a Mainer, doesn't feel the need for a platitude.

Peter is grateful for that. He hasn't got the kind of wife that will knuckle under one.

"A woman has a look of woundedness after an abortion." Mira remembers a man once telling her. She can't remember who told her that but she thinks it's a man she had an abortion by.

But Mira thinks that a woman who allows herself to inadvertently become pregnant this many times had a wounded look beforehand.

In the evening she is tired. Naturally. She is pregnant.

"I need time, not much, about 2 or 3 weeks to decide what to do," she tells her husband. "You know I didn't want a child. This was an accident. That doesn't mean you should be passing out cigars. I'm old. We have no money. There's a lot to consider."

"That's not what it's about," her husband says correctly. "I want you to have the child."

That's it. Discussion closed. He's let her know.

He doesn't talk about her fears, the fears she too is not talking about. How will I stay alive if I begin service to another? Will all my youthful creativity, my hope, my sexuality die so this being can live?

The work of it, their marriage, their commitment, all of those discussions, they are not having.

She and her husband hide volumes from each other and this is killing not only them, but the child.

Mira says to her husband, "Do you want to talk to anyone about what you're feeling, get some help?" She meant, Would you like to complain about me?

"No," he says.

Her phone rings just then. The collect call. "Yes?" she says.

"I just want to tell you I loved you."

She smiles to the phone in a blank way so that her husband cannot tell whom she is talking to. "In the past tense?" she asks.

Her husband is sitting right across from her.

"No, present. I mean love," David says, "I love you. I'm glad you told me. I thought you told me because you were going to have it, I didn't realize you were asking for support. I'm a blockhead in love," he continues.

She nods, confused to the phone. Why is she talking to the prisoner about all this and not her husband?

The prisoner then goes onto discuss the drawing class he is about to teach to people who can't draw and how they impatiently want to do faces right away, how they want to finish something.

She says, "I see" a lot to the phone and then, luckily, the Feds cut them off.

Her husband is still trying to get the weather channel on the television.

She loves her husband. She feels fondly seeing him stretched out so familiarly on the couch. His long legs that have held her up.

Her husband takes a nap and Mira goes off to meet an old boyfriend as planned. She tells the old boyfriend about everything and he encourages her to have the child by herself. Encourages her to enjoy it. The old boyfriend is stable, communicative—not wild minded like the prisoner, not remote like her husband.

She feels settled, safe, sitting there and wonders why is she torturing herself with difficult men and making her life so barren?

She sits in the sun trying to warm herself. She can hear a baby crying and she heard in her mind her husband on the phone. Both sounds are one to her . . . Earlier, a young boy had looked at her on the elevator and she had smiled at him. He shrugged back.

Her husband tells her she does not accept the wifely responsibilities. She owes him something, he says. Meaning the baby. She owes him. That's all she can hear in her mind's ear. And she thinks about the Spanish man she knew years ago who said warm things to her. That when he made love to her, he said her body was pretty. She is pretty. He loves her. Te quiro mucho. Te adoro. She wraps herself in that memory when she goes to sleep to ward off her husband's rage that he is not getting a return on his investment of marriage. That she is not delivering properly. She turns sideways when her husband makes love to her. Her face grimaces. Even though she loves him. She turns sideways. She does not come as she did so easily with the Spanish man. The Spanish man who did not come with her. Who protected himself from her. He said he loved her but he did not come.

She soothes herself on the memory of the Spanish man's kindness, gentleness, forgetting the brutal fights they had when she would not bear the responsibilities of that relationship either.

She does not love in the patriarchal way. She wants to run free.

You're too self-contained, says her husband. You don't take.

"Why do you see relationship as some kind of shopping mall?" she asks. "Why isn't it just in the moment, without all this grabbing of material existence as proof?"

"Because relationships are like that."

"What is it you want from me?" she asks presciently.

"Nothing," he lies.

The prisoner has a cigar on the bleachers and wonders what she will do. It is her last time most likely. He can offer her so little it would be understandable if she stays with her husband. She likes her husband. But something is awry there if she and he got so close in here. Something missing with the husband.

The prisoner loves his daughter. It was work at the beginning but he is glad he had his child with his ex-wife. It is an amazing thing. With love comes responsibilities. Nobody sees the responsibilities he did meet. He provided a home for them, security of a sort. He has the money for his daughter's college education. His wife needed that and he provided it. Alright, so he didn't give her himself.

Her husband must never have accepted Mira as who she is. That's why she won't surrender. Mira's husband wants her to be under his thumb. A wild thing can't be tamed. David once told Mira he would accept her as a giraffe. That's what it is. But her husband doesn't, and now she has put herself in the debate. To be the giraffe that she is, or the hippo that her husband wants her to be. Mira has made the question tangible. Everybody gets to act.

Mira hates how her body turns away from her husband when he kisses her. She can't help it. She doesn't open to him. She closes down with the sharp way he talks to her. The way he rolls his eyes when she tells him something she wants to do. The way somehow everything is her fault.

And yet she gets pregnant by him.

Her body kisses the prisoner fleetingly, on the run, on the sly, safe, she guesses, that the guards will separate them. She can move towards him. And get the hell out of there.

Her body sees a perfect infant.

And then the screen goes dead.

Perhaps all these visions aren't good.

None of her friends understand her passion for the prisoner. Think it's a joke she's played on herself. Her bad boy father returned to haunt her.

Yet the prisoner makes her laugh. Says that one can survive anything. Gives her joy, even for 10 minutes.

She needs her husband's care and love.

This care and love she has known. That shuts her down. Shuts her away.

Mira's mother never touched her. Mira can't recreate the loving feeling of a mother and child that she has never known. What Mira knows is herself as the outsider, the odd woman out, the outcast.

Now her body is clamoring to be one of the many.

Tonight she will try and respond lovingly to her husband. He is worthy of it.

She must do it.

She can't run to prison.

David is not hers, no matter how she looks at it. He belongs to the government. There will be legions of women waiting for him when he gets out.

She has to pay attention to now.

Her body is demanding it.

She has to choose whom she will love. Whom of the four of them. There were only three before. A triangle. Now there's a quadrangle. She has to choose.

Everybody in each other's hands. Everybody tangled up in her fast, quick moving hands.

TIME

He plays tennis in the yard with some inmates. They use chairs as a net. They swat hard at the ball.

Mira told him she played ping pong over the weekend and how she laughed during the long volleying because, she said, as she swatted the ball and then it so quickly came back and then so quickly she swatted again, and then it came back, . . . it was intimate, she said.

It was so wonderfully intimate.

Back and forth.

What he likes about her is that she laughs even though she is facing the end of the three weeks to decide the end of the child. Or the beginning. It could be the end of him. He knows that. His reputation is not helping anything.

And here she is telling him that even though she knows she's about to lose her hand, she finds herself laughing at the joy of smacking the ball. This is a woman who wants to live.

When he thinks about it, and he does, David is pretty sure she won't leave him. She won't be able to leave someone like him, a man who swats her back the ball, makes her smile, who reaches out to her.

She won't close that down.

"Listen," she says to her husband, "I'm going to abort. I can't have it. I don't have the temperament. I'm faithful to something else."

Her husband doesn't look at her. "When?"

"On Saturday. You don't have to come."

He says nothing. She finds that odd. "I know," she says, "it's terrible but we already agreed I wouldn't have a child and you were going to leave me. Let's stick to that. I can't have a child under these conditions."

Meaning the way he demands. Meaning her mother's leaving her. Meaning her loneliness. "I can't do that to a child," she says.

"You'd be a good mother even if you were a bad mother. You turned out fine with a bad mother."

This is fine? she wonders. Whom is he married to? "Have a child," she says, "with someone more suited to it."

Until Saturday, he says nothing more about it.

There isn't much she has left to say either.

"Saturday? Huh?" Will asks on the bleachers, puffing on his cigar. "You're going to owe it to her Davey boy. Her doing this for you."

"She's doing it for herself, not me."

"Her husband must be bullshit."

"He'll probably leave her."

"I would," Will says. "If my wife did that, I would."

"You already did leave your wife," David says. "Do you see any wives around here? I'm going to call her to see if she is okay."

"Not much you can do from here Daaaaave. Better face it. Poor kid. Jesus they're as fucked up out there as in here. Although, I'd rather have those problems. I sure would. I'd rather have an abortion this afternoon than be in here."

Will turns to see how that one went over on David only to see he isn't there and then looks across the yard and sees Dave's back running through the yard like it's a track tournament. He's going toward the telephones.

"I wonder," Will says to Clarke, "where it is he thinks he's going."

There are guys lined up thick waiting for the 3 phones. A cacophony of Spanish, Italian, English stream out at him. He sees dental floss hanging out of the mouth of one guy. The guy behind him is imitating the guy with the dental floss by hanging his sneaker by its dirty laces from his mouth. Other guys are staring off at nothing. Others jeer at the men on the phones to hurry up.

David nods to a few of them but basically he's of the Let's Get On With It school.

David looks out the window from where the phones are to the yard and there are men clustered in groups gesticulating, and David realizes how much he misses the sight of women. How they talk together so intensely. He remembers ball games and men watching vigilantly each play on the field but the women would have their heads turned, talking to the women in back of them. How women seemingly can talk forever. How Mira said that once she took a plane ride from New York to the Caribbean and two women who didn't know each other talked the entire way.

Women are so anxious to smile. Why? He should know by now because god knows he has suffered for them. Wined them, dined them, loved them, and now he is here. He gave all of them a better time than they expected and now he is here. Now he is here and has learned they just like to talk and be fondled gently and loved hard. It doesn't matter where they are. He is here and he has learned that all anyone and everyone wants is attention. All his art needs is attention. It's all attention.

She thinks he doesn't know. Mira thinks his loving one woman and thus himself would be too hard for him. He is inexperienced in the long work of it. But hasn't he learned how to hang in there with patience? Hang in and in and in and in. Don't they know what humility has been locked into him?

The prison shrink races by and pretends not to see David. After their one meeting when David told the shrink he had killed that many men in Vietnam.

Eighty men counted.

Mira told him her husband said it wasn't true because anybody who killed that many men would get a purple heart or something and apparently she asked her husband, But who would be counting?

Now she's becoming a murderess herself.

Anyway she thought he said he did get a purple heart.

David told the prison shrink that the shrink would kill too if his wife or child was being attacked. The shrink acceded to that but ended the interview.

Mira often wonders if she could make him honest. Maybe her love could salve his anger at having lost his innocence in the jungle forever. Her love could soothe his hate of himself.

She doesn't think the federal pen can.

Fact is a woman can reinstate a man better than any penal institution. All these men should be sentenced to life with strong women, those who are strong on the inside. Maybe that would make these men believe in themselves enough not to tell a lie.

She doesn't know. She had just wanted to bring some stardust into everyone's life. She just wanted to bring about a little more love in each of their lives. Her love catalyzed by David would help her love her husband who then maybe would love her and she could love David more. No one would be touching the wrong person. Everyone would just be loving. The river would be full.

Shows what she knew.

Mira seems to have written the address down wrong but finally she finds the building and Peter stops the car. He says "Good luck" as she closes her car door and smiles rather sheepishly, distracted, at him. She then turns to walk through the anti-abortion demonstrators.

She presses the 18th floor button and the door opens to a sea of young women, mostly Black, as many as if she was in an airport where all the flights had been canceled. Many of the girls are with their mothers, who are younger than Mira.

Mira gives her name to the nurse and when she says she has insurance, she gets whisked out of the sea of Black women to a fat nurse who takes her address, date of birth and date of last period while finding the time to tell Mira she writes poetry. What kind of poetry, Mira asks, as the nurse draws her blood. Even here, even now, the nurse is nursing pleasure in life.

Mira is led by the poet-nurse to the operating room, and is told to lie down on the covered seesaw bed and waits for the anesthesiologist. Another nurse scrubbed and dressed like an astronaut straps Mira down and the Indian woman doctor who is to do the abortion comes in and tells Mira her blood tests show she has gonorrhea, she who leads an amorous life in the prison of her mind. The anesthesiologist inserts the needle drip and the rest of the conversation is over.

When she wakes up, she is in another bed, a row of beds with women all in different phases of sleep or grogginess. The dark-haired woman doctor, who is Mira's age and size, is sitting next to her on her bed taking her blood pressure and says, "Oh you're awake. There was a mistake. You don't have gonorrhea." And I don't have the baby either.

The doctor rushes off on whispering shoes and Mira lies there and doesn't cry like she has other times after an abortion. She just lies there, empty.

She has done it again.

She is alone.

She does not have grief about it. She is alone. She understands that.

The anesthesia is lifting slowly, and they check her temperature and her blood flow, and now they give her juice and a cookie, and the young girls in the beds next to her, young girls like she had been once, moan in pain. Mira is used to pain.

She feels better. She sits up slowly, weakly, and puts her legs down on the linoleum floor. She pulls her clothes out awkwardly from the bag at the end of her bed and begins to dress herself. She smiles a sad, Yes, I'm okay, at the officiating nurse. "You okay enough?" the nurse asks. "Yup," Mira responds.

On woozy legs, she goes out to the still crowded waiting room and there is a white face she recognizes, her old friend, Sally. Sally takes Mira's arm and they walk slowly to the elevator. Mira raises her eyebrows to say, "That's it."

Sally says, "You did the right thing."

Mira doesn't believe that. The right thing is to say yes to life. What she did was her own thing.

They have lunch and Mira says she feels fine, really, physically. She even eats well, and they talk of these momentous decisions that you have no way of understanding but only feel your way blindly through and Sally says she herself does not regret never having children and they both remember the time when Mira took Sally for an abortion. Mira says, "Do you think it is a person?" and Sally says, "Of course not" and Mira thinks maybe Sally believes that but Mira is not sure she does. Sally says, "Let's get you to bed. You look tired."

Once she lies down, Mira wants to sleep. She can almost revive the anesthetic feeling. She is asleep as Sally lets herself out.

Asleep, dreaming about a cat with a ripped up gut when the phone rings.

"How did it go?" her husband asks.

"Fine."

He is at work, he says. "I'll see you later, then." She puts the phone down and it is then, after hearing her husband's fine, clear voice, that Mira finally cries.

The phone rings again. She turns in the bed.

Mira hears the automated voice saying there's a collect call. She pushes 9 on the phone dial pad to accept, even before she hears his voice break into the automation saying the call is from Theogenes.

"Theo," she says.

"Baby," he says. "Are you alright?"

"Yeah I am. I told you I would be."

"I want you to know you're not alone."

She is silent.

"You're not alone. I dig you too much."

But Mira, right now, isn't in the mood to fathom togetherness. She closes her eyes and holds onto the emptiness. The emptiness that is tangible. Not something imagined, wafted, sidled in and out of. She can feel it.

She turns over in her bed and listens to him gesticulating away that he's there, he's there, but her body knows he's going to come out. Her body is warning her that he'll have enough anger to put a rocketship on the moon. Her body wants to reject him.

She listens silently, empty, as her body tells her that everything will change when he gets out. They will all be in other lives. Different needs, different phases. How can he want to discuss that now?

"I'm here," David says.

"I know," she says. "Thanks."

Her husband finally comes home when it's already dark. His coming into the apartment is the part that terrifies her. He says, "I'm home," gently. Goes into the kitchen and pours himself a juice. Looks at her lying in the bed. The messy sheets. She never was a homemaker. Her dark hair the only color against all that white, the white of her face.

"You want me to get a movie?" he asks.

What she wants is forgiveness but she knows that's not coming. "If you want one," she says. She is being uncharacteristically meek. Should he trust it? He likes her this way. But it's not worth the violent means by which she gets there.

"I am sorry," she says. "I had to. We'd already decided not to . . . you know, before this happened . . ."

"You don't have to go into that now."

"Yes. But are you okay?"

He turns back to her. "It'll take me awhile to answer that question."

That's honest, she thinks. She looks over from the bed and his back is still turned to her. It was an act of self-defense on my part, she tells herself silently, but I'm still going to have to face the execution.

Two weeks later, Mira sat on the porch of the Naples Florida Ritz with her husband, his uncle and aunt. She and Peter took the trip they had planned before all this and have been up all night in their hotel room. He cannot forgive her, he says. He cannot forgive her.

Mira has picked the Ritz to take his uncle and aunt to, so as to have some beauty while she's this depressed. She does not want his relatives to have to share or see the beginning cold of the corpse of their nephew's and her relationship.

And anyway, Mira restores herself, makes herself more worthy, swirling her skirt and hearing her heels click through the hotel's marble piazza. She feels she is once again made beautiful while shining her face up to the sun next to the hotel's Italian fountain. She feels a kind of love, walking through the tiled and palm-treed lobby to the voluminous rose garden. She inhales the restoration of herself. Against the ugliness of her husband's unassailable rage.

Only hours before she had raised the topic of her having yet another child, this time she would be 46. She would do it this time.

"That's absurd," her husband said. "You've already made your decision."

"But now it could be my decision, not something that happens to me. But if I did," she breaks off into her own reverie, "where would we live? How would we carry on?" She begins the false debate to stave off the pain of losing him. Should she move to the country where her husband wants to live, should she give up her inordinate independence that so irks him, should she have a child when many her age are grandmothers. What did he think?

"I don't want to talk about it," he said "That is insane. You already made your decision."

He inhaled his cigarette, his face dour.

"You don't love me," she said.

"Fuck," he said.

This didn't stop him from being proud of her grace at lunch, her ability to always lead them to beauty.

"Why am I so odd," she asks David. "Why do I commit to nothing? My husband says that I only build spiritually. I create no lives, no edifices of love. I am on the run."

"It's because," David tells her, "you try to believe you don't desire. You tell yourself you are above desire. Desire is not to be trusted. You try to tell yourself you want nothing."

He looks seriously at her and then at the guards and then he says, "You can't lock up desire."

The next day, she stands at the top of her stairs and watches her husband carry his duffel bags down and out to the car. He is going to his house by the sea. "Don't tell anyone," he says, "that it's a split."

She nods.

"We're just figuring out what happened," he continues.

She nods.

"This anger . . . we're going to find out—" he says, and she nods then races down the stairs behind him to kiss him good-bye. He accepts the kiss, kindly. Then she races back upstairs and watches him from her window cross the street with his duffel bag.

It was as if she'd seen this scene a thousand times before in her mind. His walking away from her was always inevitable, always what she had been waiting to see before her.

"Thank the child," someone said to her. "Thank the child for catalyzing your freedom."

What freedom?

Her husband said the night before he went, he said what he must have rehearsed a hundred times in his car. "I can't accept the sadness of it. I can't accept living the life you want. A life of your mind. I've got no other choice."

She tells herself that one day he will thank her. For his freedom. Maybe not. He too has to find love, the long haul of it in his own prison. She, too, she doesn't know if she will find love, the long haul of it, but her soul keeps pulsing forward, making its own illogical demands. And she does heed it. A blind faithfulness, if that.

David tells her he has no faith that their love will work. She is not wild enough for him.

"You're right," she responded. "I hate chaos."

"I'm worried," he said, "that you want a safe relationship."

"You should be," she said, "because I do."

"We're in a relationship," he said.

"That's true."

"Do you trust it?" he asked.

"It was loving of me to let my husband go to a woman who can give him what he wants."

"You think I love you?" David asked.

"You love that I accept you as you are. I'm the only woman you know who's not angry at you. That's because I don't want anything from you. But now I might. And now I might get angry."

"I know," he said, "who you really are."

She shuddered and gripped his hand.

"Maybe," she said. "I told my husband that I never shared myself with him but I would try. I would tell him what I feel, I said. That would be the movement forward. So I told him that I needed my inner life to come first. And then he asked for a divorce. That's what can come of knowing me," she said to David. "You'll want a divorce.

"All I care about now is that I speak. But when you do speak, the thing is, you pay the cost. Being yourself David has its cost."

"You think I don't know that?"

"Yeah. You know that. My husband too. I hadn't realized how full of suffering it all is. How so for all of us. To be ourselves. What a risk of loneliness it is to be ourselves. And yet the loneliness of not being ourselves is worse. We're fucked, you know that?"

"That's why we have sex."

She smiled. "We have sex?"

"We will baby, we will."

"Prison sex, you mean."

"Whatever you want to call it," he said. "It's what we're having. To not be fucked."

She scratched her neck and smiled to the wall. "The thing is," she said, "I feel great."

He nodded. "Why do you think that is?"

"I don't know. Maybe I did even the wrong thing but I did what I thought I had to do. That, what's inside you, needs little else. Even if you hurt, I feel," she continued, "like I don't know where I'm going or why, but I'm myself."

"The road to wisdom is paved with excess."

"You would know that quote," she answers. "Anyway, the exact quote is 'the road of excess leads to the palace of wisdom.'"

"Yeah, well being yourself is the kind of excess he's talking about. Your husband is a nice guy, but he wanted to cage you. I don't."

"Hmmm . . ."

"No, I don't."

"You can't. That's the real reason, if any, we'll have sex. Because you can't cage me."

"I don't want to baby. But you better stay faithful till I get out." He laughs.

"I gotta go to prison too? I didn't do anything wrong."

"Yup. You gotta be faithful."

"Why don't I become your third wife?" she says just to create some distance.

"Forget it. I want to keep you. I lose all my wives."

"What happened to Susan?"

"I told her I am not interested in her in that way. And I'm not."

"Do you think your ex-wife will want you back?"

"I don't know. But I don't look in the rear view mirror. I'm going forward when I get out. With you, honey."

"Maybe I'll be faithful." However, she has no intention of it. He wouldn't be faithful either if she was in jail. Hell, she wonders if he would be faithful if he was out of jail.

But right now, she doesn't care. She will be faithful to herself. And that may, or it may not, involve being faithful to him. It won't be her decision.

It'll be her desire.

Her long time desire.

That was in the end what she chose for.

FREEDOM

It was Pearl Harbor Day, December 7th, but the weather was shockingly warm in the Northeast. Mira wore black pants and a velvet halter-top, as if it was summer. Her hair washed, high heels, she began driving to the outskirts of New Jersey. It was two years later and she was picking David up from jail. She and Peter had separated two years before that.

She parked in the parking lot of FCI Fort Dix and waited. He was supposed to walk out and be cleared around ten a.m. It was only marijuana growing, stupid but not violent, yet it was the Rockefeller Drug Laws and he had ended up serving ten years in a Federal prison.

As she waited in the car, she thought about how his sculpture had won him grants, he did have a purple heart from Vietnam, how he'd made $50,000 a week with his marijuana business, in other words, he was a total character and how here she was, waiting to pick him up, her life entwined with his, because she had been so fascinated at the trajectory of his life. All those letters and visits and soon the whole impossibility of never having sex had made the whole thing impossibly sexy.

She was picking him up to drive him to a month in a halfway house, the next step in his emancipation.

Then she saw him tall, in a white t-shirt, slacks, walking through the cars, looking for her blue Escort, ten years since she had seen him walking outside of a contained visiting room. Here he was in normal clothes, nobody around him, carrying the paintings he had done in prison neatly tied in a roll, next to his duffel bag.

"Hey baby," he said, laughing, as she jumped out of the car, standing in the sunlight, looking at him.

She didn't know what to say.

"My god," she said. "Are you sure you don't want to go back in?"

"Let's get out of here."

They drove and he looked out the window, hard. They held hands. "Do you want a coffee? Something?" she asked.

"No thanks."

"I'll take you to lunch after you see my place," she said, "somewhere nice in the city."

He had often talked about hating the food in prison. "Last night," he told her, "the Italian guys made a huge dinner with white napkins as a goodbye party for me. Tomatoes. It was something. I wonder where they got the vegetables."

She smiled.

"Well at least today," she said, "you won't be using plastic forks and knives."

He laughed. "Yeah," as if it was almost not possible.

She knew pretty soon they would see the back of the Statue of Liberty and she had always cried when she passed it returning from visiting him. Sometimes she had been so turned on by being locked up in the visiting room with him, his hard body as they say, his romantic words, his charm and intelligence, that driving home from a visit she had masturbated in the car. One time she had been thrown out of the visiting room for the way his big hand kept stroking her back, her neck, her legs.

Do you think we have chemistry? he'd asked her then.

They parked in New York in her garage and she brought him upstairs. He walked through her old walk-up apartment, with its French doors and slanting floors, like it was a palace. He looked out the windows at Second Avenue and the hubbub. The trucks, the people racing by, people talking, talking. He looked out the back windows at the garden below that four apartment buildings shared, next to a school.

He took it all in. She came up next to him and they hugged. Then they began kissing. And then they went to her bed. They lay down together and he undressed her, on top of the comforter. He began kissing her body. The last time she had been in bed with someone in this bed was with Peter. A long time ago. She felt strange. But here he was, big and in perfect shape, beautiful, really, and she was happy he was finally here in her arms, naked.

"I can't fucking believe it," he said.

"Don't worry about it."

"Never happened to me before."

"Don't worry about it. Everything is so loaded. You're probably in some kind of shock. Anyway ten years of foreplay has a touch of pressure," she said.

Then she suggested the urban solution to all problems, "Come on let's go to a restaurant. We can table this," she said laughing. "Believe me I am not too worried."

She knew there was enough sexuality in him that this was nothing to even think about. It was just the day, the strangeness of this day.

They got dressed. Apparently, he once told her, in the old days before he went to prison they'd had sex together in their twenties when she lived by a cove, but she hardly remembered it. She only recalled how he had left her a poem the next morning on the typewriter that faced out over an ever-changing grey and blue sea. She never forgot his handwriting and the fact he would do that. She didn't remember him in bed. And, for obvious reasons, actual sex had never been a big part of their current relationship, with her visiting him once a month in prison. Just sex in the mind and she often wondered if she preferred it that way anyway.

She took him to Il Cantinori, on Tenth. Enormous flower arrangements, windows over the streets, white tablecloths, even for lunch. It was elegant and he had salmon and wine and her best friend who knew him too showed up with clothes for him and even underwear and she wondered about that but they were all excited about his freedom and seeing him out of prison khakis and what was he going to do and he gave many unrealistic answers and nobody cared, just the happiness at all of them never having to see that prison again.

After the dessert, the gaiety, she said, "Listen, I've gotta drive to you to Boston now. You have to be there by sundown. You can't be late."

Once they retrieved his duffel bag, she and he got back in the car and they drove the long way from New York. They held hands and he talked about how much he loved her and what their future would be. That she was the one and she didn't really believe it but she was like that with all men anyway, she didn't believe much of what any of them said, not because she thought they were lying but she knew how very much everything changes.

They got to Lowell where the halfway house was, they got there early. No way he was going to check in a second before he had to.

"What shall we do?"

"Let's park in that bar's parking lot down the street."

They did and that's when she ended up on top of him in her tiny car, making love with him, lustfully, passionately, happily, who cared who could see them, nobody seemed to be out in Lowell on a weekday afternoon in this part of town and all systems worked as they say and years later he gave her a framed photo of that parking lot as a gift.

It was a long seduction.

They had a passionate affair, but they did not really get on, she was too serious and he was a bit of a wheeler-dealer and so they once again became friends, just as they had been during those ten years of visits, and twenty years of youth before.

Peter took up yoga classes to stop smoking once he moved into his house by the sea, after he and Mira split up.

At yoga, he met two women as romantic possibilities. He went out with one of them and he told Mira that when he was annoyed with this young woman, he'd blurt out, "Mira, I don't agree."

But this new woman loved him and she, like him, had moved from New York to the sea town, and she, like him, wanted a life that was community and beauty and away from the madness and ambition of a city. They became lovers and he moved in with her right away.

He started helping the new woman in his life fix up her little shop. He made repairs in it, building shelves and tables, as he had done for Mira when they were married. He wanted to call Mira to tell her his dreams because she was good at that kind of thing, she had an intricate probing mind, but his girlfriend said,

"No, you do that with me now." Soon he was not allowed to see Mira except with his girlfriend there. The three of them would meet, and sometimes Mira brought David, whose handsomeness would be a topic of discussion for Peter's girlfriend. It was awkward for Mira but she understood that she and Peter were committed to forging a friendship after marriage. They knew something about each other that no one else would ever know. They knew how they had lived a long time in loneliness. They had both not been parented and only they knew the suffering that comes with that.

Finally Peter asked the new girlfriend if she would have a child. His marriage had broken up over his wife refusing to have a child. It was important to him and he was getting near his late 40s.

The girlfriend wasn't sure but she knew how to love, and she liked a domestic life, and she came from money, and they did not need his carpentry earnings to educate the child and so she said yes.

Soon they had a child.

Peter was ecstatic. We are pregnant, he said.

Nine months later, Peter sent Mira a photo of the little girl's hand when she was born.

The four would visit regularly, Mira, Peter, the daughter and the girlfriend. The little girl would dance around her father's legs. "He's mine," she'd say to Mira.

"I know," Mira said, oddly falling in love with the daughter. That was a surprise for all of them.

She found she also never stopped loving her husband's sensitivity and goodness and true north-ness and they both were shocked that he never stopped loving her intelligence and her being what he called "a freedom fighter." He respected that she had given him the freedom to have a child and to find the kind of love from a wife that he needed, and she had asked for no money when they divorced, "You'll need it for your family."

He realized she'd methodically ensured he got what he wanted. He knew she did that in her inverted sense of love. And he knew, better than anyone, that what was behind it was she did not feel she deserved love for herself and she would never bring anyone down with her.

Peter, the girlfriend, and the daughter who also came to love Mira, came to stay each year in Mira's apartment, some of it to see New York, and some to cement their relationship. Mira, Peter and the little girl would go ice-skating (the mother would walk to the rink for her exercise). As Peter and Mira skated in circles to Nat King Cole, with the daughter a little ahead of them, he would tell Mira he was grateful for those years of freedom with Mira. That was how he could take being so roped in now.

Mira felt a bit proud and then fell on the ice and cracked her shoulder. She got up as if nothing had happened. It would heal (and it did) and she took it as just part of how she must pay for how she hurt everyone.

They all found it odd how Mira loved the daughter, the presents she gave her, the games they played together when the daughter was small, how Mira and the daughter did things together. Once they even went to Quebec City together and Mira and the little seven-year-old girl walked past a sex shop.

"Look," the daughter said, "a toy shop."

Mira spirited her past the shop and laughingly told the mother and Peter. The mother cried tears of love for her daughter. Both the mother and Mira felt that way.

What a strange bond but it was forged and every year Mira also made sure to stay with them when she was by the sea.

They were, in a way, family.

Mira did turn out to be committed to Peter after all.

And something in Peter and his girlfriend understood that.

Even the girl, when she grew up, understood it too.

Mira was a woman that men liked—she was fun, usually not interested in the mundane, and she liked being a girl. So it was surprising that she never married again.

She and David had tried to have a relationship and then, one day, on Block Island, they were having dinner by the harbor.

"What are you reading?" she asked.

"I don't have time to read. I could do that in the klink."

She nodded, understanding that his life was about rebuilding himself and making up for what he lost financially. His passion, when not working, was mostly golf. Golf relaxed him.

He told her, the head of the golf club had said to him, "I didn't know you were retired."

He wasn't but he played every day.

David tried to get her to marry him and create a normal life but it turned out that she was the real outlier of the three. She had no desire for a suburban life of golf and dinner parties discussing construction changes on people's houses.

It didn't suit her.

David got annoyed with her, no woman had ever refused him anything before and eventually David met a woman who played tennis who switched to golf for him, and why not, and a few years later they married.

"I owe it to her to make her feel secure," he told Mira, and Mira was moved at his sensitivity to this woman.

"But why didn't you tell me? I thought we were friends," she asked. "I had to hear it through gossip."

"You were the hardest person for me to tell."

They got over that, too.

Mira would visit the sea town where both David and Peter lived with their new women and David showed her his new house on the sea. He had become affluent, this man who made money growing marijuana was good at making money legally, too. His wife was not there when he brought Mira over, she was working. Mira, as always, walked to the bookshelves.

"Oh, it's my work," she said, looking through his books.

He joined her at the bookshelf and opened a book and passed it to her. She saw stories she'd sent him in prison.

She wanted to cry.

The house seemed empty of life except for her books and his paintings. The wife, she thought, can't be that interesting and that is why he hides her.

"Do you need money?" he asked.

"I always need money," she said.

Three months later he sent her a check for $2000. She did need it.

Mira worked at various types of literary engagements, all of them insecure, but she enjoyed them. Her mind had to be active.

She met a man she liked who said, "I can't imagine you married."

She wondered what he meant.

She was to find out he couldn't imagine himself married, at least not to her. And maybe he had seen, early on, she was not easy in love.

But they continued seeing each other, respecting each other's privacy, it was Rilke who said that lovers must protect each other's solitude, and she and this man, Kurt, did protect each other's solitude. They saw each other twice a week and kept their different homes.

She enjoyed his exuberances and he was smart and she did not get bored with him. He, too, read all the time. He, similar to her, liked jazz. They never argued and maybe it was because they did not live together or marry, even though she would never admit it to him. It hurt her he was not as in love with her as David and Peter had been. She ascribed it to her no longer having her full beauty. But she also had to admit that, when she had been married, she had continually written in her journals, "I need more time alone."

She had now got it.

Yet it gnawed at Mira's pride that Kurt did not want to live with her. "Why don't you?" she'd ask.

"I need time to be alone to renew myself." In some deep way, she understood and identified with him in that, even though it made her feel ancillary and not desired.

The irony, she thought. Kurt was like her and she was like Peter now. She was the one wanting more connection.

Peter sometimes called to say his new wife was controlling and she'd complain that Kurt was too independent of her.

When she asked David how his marriage was, he said, "You know how it is, you become like brother and sister."

She laughed.

No matter what any of them said, they knew, in each of their hearts, in truth they had exactly what they needed and they were free.

And each one of them knew what they had lost to get there.

And, in the mornings when David drove his truck to a construction site in the seacoast sun, sipping his coffee, his dog beside him, his heart felt large and joyful. When Peter watched his daughter who was much like him play soccer and get annoyed at a lost shot, as he had when he had been a young athlete, and she got into his car after and slammed the door in anger, he smiled at her, full of love and the freedom of knowing, really knowing her. His daughter would not leave him, as his parents had, as his first wife had. She was his.

And when Mira took her computer to the Polish coffeeshop and the Polish waitress, her own age, immediately brought over a sliced banana and coffee, and it was cold out, but early morning and Mira dove into her stories, while overhearing the Polish waitress saying she was going to retire and Mira reflected that obviously the Polish waitress had been smarter with money than Mira, but still, still, Mira was lost, gone into the possibilities in her stories and the life there, and she too could not imagine ever leaving that.

She put her hand over her face as she tried to think up the next sentence, and it drifted across her mind, randomly, that this life was no longer prison sex, it was every moment sex.

THE END

ABOUT THE AUTHOR

British born, Montreal raised, New York City honed, JACQUELINE GAY WALLEY, under the pen name GAY WALLEY, has been publishing short stories since 1988 and published her first novel, *Strings Attached*, with University Press of Mississippi (1999), which was a Finalist for the Pirates Alley/Faulkner Award and earned a Writer's Voice Capricorn Award and the Paris Book Festival Award. *The Erotic Fire of the Unattainable: Aphorisms on Love, Art and the Vicissitudes of Life* was published by IML Publications in 2007 and was reissued by Skyhorse Publishing 2015. This book, *The Erotic Fire of the Unattainable* was a finalist for the Paris Book Festival Award and from this, she wrote a screenplay for the film, *The Unattainable Story* (2016) with actor, Harry Hamlin, which premiered at the Mostra Film Festival in Sao Paolo, Brazil. Walley also wrote a screenplay for director Frank Vitale's docufiction feature film, *Erotic Fire of the Unattainable: Longing to be Found* (2020), which was featured in Brooklyn Film Festival, Sarasota Film Festival, Cinequest Film & Creativity Festival in San Jose, ReadingFilmFest, and American Fringe in Paris (2020). Her novel, *Lost in Montreal* (2013) was published by Incanto Press, along with the novel, *Duet*, which was written with Kurt Haber. Walley's e-books, *How to Write Your First Novel*, *Save Your One Person Business from Extinction*, and *The Smart Guide to Business Writing* are featured on Bookboon, as well as *How to Keep Calm*

and Carry on Without Money and *How to be Beautiful* available on Amazon. In 2013, her play *Love, Genius and a Walk* opened in the Midtown Festival, New York, and was nominated for 6 awards including best playwright, in 2018, it also played in London at The Etcetera Theatre above The Oxford Arms pub as well as at three other pub theatres. It is scheduled to open in 2021 in Theatro Techni in London. October 2021, Jacqueline Gay Walley's 6 novel *Venus as She Ages Collection: Strings Attached* (second edition, under her pen name, Gay Walley), *To Any Lengths*, *Prison Sex*, *The Bed You Lie In*, *Write She Said*, and *Magnetism*, is being launched worldwide through IML Publications, distributed by Ingram.

Since IML's humble erratic beginnings, the mascot, which has reverently danced across our newsletter, the watermarks of the website, the original interiors, and now these front and back pages, is a graphic symbol of the Kalahari San Bushmen's Trickster God, the praying mantis, who has forever—or for as long as they can remember—been inspiring the mythological stories of these First People who nomadically walk the earth whenever they can, as our nomad authors write their way through life.

CPSIA information can be obtained
at www.ICGtesting.com
Printed in the USA
BVHW072046260921
617573BV00005B/67

9 781955 314077